On the Corner of Coetze and Klein

A Chance Meeting, A Love That Defied Expectations!

By

Judi Moreo

Turning Point International

Las Vegas, Nevada

Table of Contents

Prologue

I never intended to set foot in Africa. The entire trip was supposed to be a prank on my friend Vimmi—a joke that, in hindsight, took a costly and unexpected turn. At the time, I couldn't have imagined how that impulsive decision would set my life on an entirely new trajectory.

I certainly didn't expect to meet a man at the corner of Coetze and Klein, one even more handsome than Tom Selleck at his best – nor did I ever expect him to capture my heart.

That day marked the beginning of a journey that would rewrite my story. What started as an impulsive, humorous detour became a transformative chapter of my life filled with unexpected passion and profound connection. I had come to Africa with nothing more than a light heart and a sense of mischief, yet I left with a heart fuller than I ever could have imagined, captured by a man who unexpectedly became my destiny.

Chapter 1
The Corner of Coetze and Klein

The early afternoon sun in Johannesburg cast warm, golden rays across the sidewalk when I first arrived downtown, bathing the hustle and bustle in a gentle glow that made every surface shimmer. I paused momentarily to take it in—the angled light catching in the windows of passing cars, dancing along the polished granite of nearby buildings, and reflecting off the tinted office windows overhead. Traffic streamed past in an almost choreographed flow: cars, black taxis (minibuses), and the occasional motorcycle wove through lanes with varying degrees of grace. The clamor of engines, horns, and squeaking brakes intermingled in a discordant symphony that felt brash one second and oddly rhythmic the next.

At the corner of Coetze and Klein, a traffic light stood poised to change from red to green. A crowd of pedestrians—including me—had converged there in an impatient knot. Some tapped their feet or scrolled through their phones, while others stood, lost in thought or conversation. I shifted my weight from one foot to the other, acutely aware of the small camera bag strapped diagonally across my torso. The concierge at my hotel had been adamant that I keep any valuables out of view. Even with the strap wound securely around my shoulder and my passport stuffed into my boot, I still felt like a beacon of foreignness, as though every passerby could sense the unfamiliar tension in my posture.

As I waited for the light to change, I was hyperaware of the faintest details: the grizzled texture of the sidewalk beneath my boots, the swirl of unfamiliar accents around me, and the scratchy dryness of the late afternoon air. There was a swirl of new and unexpected scents, too—some floral, some spicy, a hint of diesel exhaust, and maybe something like hot concrete. It all mingled to create a layered tapestry of aromas that spoke of a city humming with life at every corner.

People surged around me as a minibus taxi approached the curb. Its door slid open, releasing a handful of passengers who joined the mass at the intersection. A small group of teenage girls chattered excitedly in a language I couldn't place, perhaps Zulu or Sotho. Nearby, a young woman in a headscarf rifled through her purse, searching for something while keeping an eye on the traffic. An older gentleman in a tweed suit shuffled past me, muttering under his breath. All this motion and sound created a gentle press of bodies, and each time someone drifted too near, I felt my heart flutter with renewed caution. I tightened my grip on my camera bag, comforted by its firm feel against my ribs.

The buildings that rose around me were colossal blocks of concrete and glass. Some had seen better days, their façades dull or discolored from decades of urban wear and tear. Others gleamed with modern sophistication, reflecting the afternoon sun like sleek mirrors. The reflection captivated me: dusty pinks, vibrant oranges, and that soft purple hue one sees only in certain corners of southern Africa. It felt as if the entire city was quietly setting the stage for some vivid spectacle where every color played a role.

When the light finally shifted, we began to cross. The crowd swept forward collectively, and I moved with it. My mind was already drifting ahead, thinking of where I might head next—perhaps a museum or a quick detour into one of the many side streets I'd passed on my ride from the airport. But then, something tugged at the corner of my vision: a bright splash of crimson down the road to my left.

A café, its broad terrace decked out in red umbrellas, caught my attention like a beacon amid the slate-gray buildings. Even from a distance, I could see a scattering of iron chairs and small round tables, each neatly arranged beneath those cheerful umbrellas. A gentle breeze caught the fabric overhead, creating a rippling effect that seemed almost to wave me over. After nearly twenty hours of travel—economy class, my body felt stiff, and my mind felt even more so. A pang of longing spread through my chest at the sight of that café. It promised comfort: a hot beverage, a quiet seat, and maybe a chance to more leisurely watch this new city whirl around me.

I realized with a start that a traffic cop was blowing his whistle farther down the street. Cars lurched forward, and pedestrians shifted to avoid them. The sudden jolt of awareness reminded me that Johannesburg was known for its dynamism and unpredictability. Somewhere in my head, I heard the concierge's voice reminding me to stay vigilant. My hand instinctively closed around the strap of my camera bag.

As I reached the curb on the other side of the intersection, I felt a light but insistent tap on my shoulder. Every cautionary tale I'd heard about big city theft or distraction scams rushed to the forefront of my mind, and my heartbeat skittered. The next second, I was half-turned, braced for confrontation, the corners of my vision hazy with adrenaline.

"Excuse me," came a voice—deep, resonant, and surprisingly polite.

I stared at the man who'd tapped me, my breath caught in my throat. He was tall, maybe six foot two, with broad shoulders that filled out his tailored suit. The suit was immaculately cut: the lines crisp, the fabric expensive. His thick, dark hair was neatly styled—short on the sides, a bit longer on top. It gave him a polished yet approachable look. But it was his eyes that truly made me pause. They were a deep, warm brown, carrying a hint of laughter, as though he could sense my tension and found a gentle way to acknowledge it.

In that split second, I hesitated. Should I run? Should I bolt into the crowd? Then I noticed the slight lift at the corner of his mouth and a calmness in his gaze that belied any threat. My shoulders loosened, though my guard was still up.

He spoke again, his accent lilting. The words came out in a smooth cascade, and in my jet-lagged haze, I initially failed to construe them as English. I only caught a few distinct syllables and felt my cheeks flush.

"I'm sorry," I blurted out, my voice sharper than I intended. I shook my head to clear my confusion. "I only speak English."

He smiled then, a kind of patient amusement lighting up his face. "I was speaking English," he said gently. "I said, I've been running up and down this street for half an hour trying to find someone who knows you so they could introduce us. No luck. So here I am... introducing myself."

I blinked in astonishment, my grip on my camera bag loosening a fraction. Behind us, pedestrians jostled around, swerving to avoid our little tableau. A car horn blared somewhere, followed by another whistle from the traffic cop. The man nodded toward the café I'd been eyeing.

"I realize this is forward," he continued, "but would you like to join me for a coffee?"

A snort of laughter escaped me before I could stop it—part disbelief, part nervous reflex. The notion that this tall, striking stranger had been looking to meet me in a city of millions was so improbable it bordered on ridiculous. And yet, it also carried a dash of that delightful, impossible serendipity you sometimes crave when traveling.

I found myself giving him a second, more careful look. The sunlight caught the faint shadow of stubble along his jaw. He seemed very much like someone who had stepped out of a glossy travel magazine—handsome, yes, but with a magnetic presence amplified by his quiet confidence. No immediate alarm buzzed in my head, and there was no sense that I needed to flee. If anything, I felt intrigued, like I had stumbled into the beginning of some unexpected adventure.

"I—uh—sure," I heard myself say, my voice wavering slightly.

He extended his hand, broad palm up, an invitation and a courtesy all at once. "Jeff Holman," he introduced himself, his smile revealing straight white teeth. "Originally from Rhodesia—Zimbabwe now—but I've been here in South Africa for a while."

I took his hand, finding his grip warm and surprisingly comforting. "Nice to meet you, Jeff.

I'm—" My caution flared again. Was it safe to give my real name? But the city was busy, the sun was still high enough to keep things well-lit, and hiding at this particular moment felt unnecessary. "I'm Sarah," I finished at last, trying to keep my voice steady.

With that, Jeff deftly guided us across the street toward the café. He had a certain elegance in how he moved, weaving between the pedestrians who poured out of taxis and buses, and I caught a hint of a spicy cologne as he walked. I followed close behind, still internally grappling with whether this was a good decision. Yet the café, with its inviting terrace of red umbrellas, drew us in like a quiet sanctuary from the roaring cityscape.

As we stepped onto the terrace, I noticed more details: the wrought-iron fence marking the boundary between café and sidewalk, the potted plants near the entrance that added a touch of greenery to the urban setting. The chairs looked delicate—filigreed backs with swirling designs— but it felt sturdy when I brushed my hand across one. Small glass vases holding single bright blooms of local flowers sat on each table, a cheerful burst of color.

A waiter in a crisp white shirt and black apron greeted us with a polite nod. Jeff asked for a table outside, gesturing to one tucked beneath an extensive umbrella. I sank into one of the chairs, pleased to find it surprisingly comfortable, and took in the street scene anew. The vantage point was different from here—slightly above the sidewalk level, giving me a better view of the passing crowd.

The city felt alive: men in business attire hurrying toward a late meeting, women with stylish handbags weaving through the foot traffic, and young couples sharing quiet jokes as they strolled hand in hand. The swirl of languages constantly reminded us of Johannesburg's diverse tapestry. I picked out a snippet of English here, an Afrikaans phrase there, and at least two or three languages I'd never heard spoken before.

Jeff settled across from me, unbuttoning the single button on his suit jacket as he sat. "You're traveling alone?" he asked, his voice warm with curiosity.

I nodded, smoothing a wrinkle in my jacket before folding my hands in my lap. "Yes. I arrived yesterday," I explained. "I wanted to see Johannesburg first—maybe for a few days—then head to Kruger National Park or Cape Town. Honestly, I'm still figuring out my itinerary."

He inclined his head thoughtfully, his eyes never leaving my face. "Both destinations are incredible and very different from each other. Kruger for the wildlife, Cape Town for the ocean, and the wine farms." He paused, and then a hint of a grin touched his lips. "If you decide on Kruger, I might be able to offer some advice. I've made a few safaris in my time."

On the Corner of Coetze and Klein

Before I could respond, the waiter returned with menus, accompanied by the comforting aroma of freshly ground coffee. I lifted the menu, scanning the offerings—lattes, cappuccinos, espressos—some local specialties with names that sounded enticing but unfamiliar. I decided on a cappuccino, feeling I needed something creamy and substantial to offset my jet lag. Jeff ordered an Americano, then politely handed the menus back.

Jeff leaned forward the moment the waiter left, a thoughtful crease on his brow. "So, Sarah, what made you choose Johannesburg as your starting point?"

His question hung in the air, and I exhaled slowly, trying to explain my motivations. "There's a vibrant history here," I began. "I mean, the city's gone through so many transformations—gold rush days, the apartheid era, the new democracy… I've read about the cultural shift, the art scene, and all these changes that seem to happen in real-time. It felt like a place where the future is always around the corner, you know?"

He nodded, a flicker of admiration lighting his features. "That's a good way to put it," he said. "Johannesburg can be gritty, but it's alive like some other cities aren't. It's constantly reinventing itself."

I felt myself relax at his words. There was a sincerity in his tone that reassured me, a sense that he, too, had come to appreciate the city's contradictory blend of promise and difficulty. "I'm

15

hoping to do a tour of Soweto. But I also want time to wander and explore alone—take photographs, soak in the atmosphere."

Jeff regarded me carefully. "Well, if you're interested in photography, you're in luck. Johannesburg is a city of hidden gems. You can walk down one street and see nothing but rundown warehouses. Then you turn a corner and find a mural stretching three stories high or a pop-up market selling handcrafted goods from half a dozen African countries."

I leaned back in my chair, imagining the photographic possibilities. Already, I regretted that I had not taken more street shots as I walked. Perhaps after coffee, I'd roam around a bit more.

When the drinks arrived, the café's ambiance enveloped us in a soft hum. The cappuccino was served in a generously sized cup with a mountain of foam and a dusting of cocoa on top. Jeff's Americano came in a sleek white mug, steam curling upward in lazy tendrils. We paused to take our first sips. My cappuccino was divine—rich, smooth, perfectly balanced. The warmth spread through my hands and down into my core, easing away the stiffness in my neck from hours on a plane.

"Now, this is exactly what I needed," I murmured, letting the moment sink in. The swirl of city sounds around us felt slightly distant as if the café's terrace was a cocoon of relative calm amid the chaos.

On the Corner of Coetze and Klein

Jeff chuckled softly. "Nothing quite like a good cup of coffee after a long trip," he said. "I remember my first time stepping off a plane in Johannesburg. The airport was different then—smaller, less modern—but I'll never forget how the air smelled. It was a mix of dust, heat, and ... possibility." He set his mug down, eyes drifting to the street as if recalling a memory. "I felt like a new chapter was starting."

I found myself smiling at that, understanding all too well. Traveling sometimes felt like flipping the page to a fresh part of life, each place holding its own stories and lessons. "What brought you here from Zimbabwe?" I asked, curious to know more about his background.

He hesitated, a thoughtful expression crossing his face. "Civil unrest. We stayed through the transition to Zimbabwe, but times got tough. He shrugged as if to wave away any deeper complexities. "Johannesburg has been good to me. I'm in import/export, so it's a prime spot."

I nodded. There was a note in his voice—a slight wistfulness suggesting a history he might not be ready to share. That was okay. I had my complexities, too, and we'd only met now.

The conversation lulled momentarily as we both took another sip of our drinks. Beyond terrace, the city carried on its performance: the beep of reversing trucks, the squeal of bus brakes, the distant clang of construction equipment.

17

Pedestrians paused at the same intersection I'd been at minutes before, waiting for their turn to cross. A couple strolled by, the woman's laughter bright as the man gestured animatedly. It was mesmerizing to watch these little vignettes of life unfolding in real-time.

"I still can't believe you walked up to me in the middle of all this," I said, grinning slightly at Jeff over the rim of my cup. My earlier nerves were ebbing away, replaced by a cautious but genuine curiosity. "I mean, I guess I do stand out, but it's still... bold."

He laughed a low, pleasant rumble. "Maybe a bit," he conceded. "But fortune favors the bold, right? Plus, there was something about how you looked at the city. It's as if you saw it for the first time—both eager and overwhelmed. I remember that feeling. So I thought, why not say hello?"

A blush crept into my cheeks, but I tried to mask it by glancing at my coffee. "I suppose that's exactly how I feel," I admitted. "Part eager, part overwhelmed."

"I'd be happy to help tilt the balance more toward 'eager,' if you'll let me," Jeff said, leaning in slightly, his brown eyes twinkling. "I can give you a local's perspective—show you some neighborhoods you might not venture into on your own, introduce you to local cuisine, maybe even help you pick out a few spots that'll make for great photographs."

On the Corner of Coetze and Klein

The suggestion made my heart skip. A stranger, yes, but also someone who exuded an easygoing warmth and confidence that hinted at reliability. Still, a voice in my head—the cautious traveler side—reminded me that trusting too readily could be a mistake. Yet another part of me wanted to embrace the spontaneity of this encounter. Wasn't that part of the reason I traveled in the first place?

"I'll think about it," I said, keeping my tone friendly but noncommittal. "I appreciate the offer."

He nodded as if he recognized my need to hold onto a measure of control. "Of course," he said. "You've just arrived, and you're dealing with the city's intensity. Take your time. If you want to explore independently first, I get it."

Somehow, that understanding put me even more at ease. I glanced around at the café once again, noticing a few details I'd missed: the black-and-white tiled floor leading into the interior, the small chalkboard menu near the entrance that boasted daily specials in neat handwriting, and a subtle soundtrack playing overhead—soft African jazz that gently blended with the street noise.

As I took another sip, I let the caffeine work its magic. The tension in my spine started to melt away, and my senses sharpened. I could taste the mild sweetness in the foam, feel the gentle swirl of the breeze against my cheeks, and hear the faint conversation of other customers nearby. A trio of friends behind us laughed uproariously at some joke while two older women at another table chatted in hushed tones, glancing occasionally at a newspaper.

"This is your first time in Africa?" Jeff asked after a moment, carefully gauging how much he could ask without prying.

"Yes," I said, my voice lifting a bit. "I've dreamed about coming here for years—mostly to see the wildlife and experience the culture. I've always loved photography, and the idea of capturing wild animals on film… well, it felt like a calling."

"You'll find plenty to photograph here," he assured me. "Not only the animals — also people, neighborhoods, food. Even the way the light hits the city in the early morning or late afternoon can be breathtaking."

I raised an eyebrow. "You sound like a photographer yourself."

He chuckled. "Hardly. But I've spent enough years living here to notice. If you pay attention, Joburg can be quite beautiful when it wants to be. It doesn't always reveal that beauty in obvious ways."

I liked that phrasing—it made Johannesburg sound like a character in a story that chose when to show you its best side. I took a long look at Jeff, noticing the flecks of gold in his brown eyes and how a faint line appeared between his brows when he was thinking. There was a confidence about him, yes, but also a sense of lived experience. The sun was rising higher now, painting the edges of his jaw with a honeyed glow.

Chapter 2
First Impressions

"Tell me about yourself," Jeff said, leaning forward with his arms folded neatly on the small café table. His voice was quiet yet full of warmth that instantly bridged the gap between us. The hustle of Johannesburg's busy downtown framed our little conversation bubble, with the clatter of cups and saucers keeping an energetic tempo. Despite the buzz of the city, Jeff's gaze was steady— an invitation that made me feel like the only person in the world at that moment. He had this open, attentive way about him, like he was genuinely curious and waiting to be surprised. "How did you end up all alone in Johannesburg?"

I hesitated, a subtle mix of nerves and excitement fluttering in my chest. My fingers toyed with the hem of my napkin, and I felt the edges of my lips curve into a small, uncertain smile. It wasn't that I was shy or ashamed—though, I suppose a part of me was embarrassed at how spontaneous (or reckless, depending on your point of view) my story sounded. It was more that every time I recounted the chain of events that landed me here, I ended up marveling at my boldness and the strangeness of fate. Over the past few days, I'd told the "short version" of my tale to flight attendants, a customs officer, and the hotel clerk who handed me my room key. Yet, saying it to Jeff—this stranger who radiated kindness—felt different. I wanted to share more than a canned summary. I wanted to show him the excitement, the chaos, and the nerve-wracking leap of faith behind each twist.

"Well," I said, clearing my throat as I began at the beginning, "I have this friend—Vimmi. He's a photographer in Las Vegas, where I live. He started as one of the models in a fashion show I produced a couple of years ago, and we hit it off. The next thing I knew, he became the official photographer for my agency and then a kind of…partner in crime, I guess you could say. Vimmi's the type who can turn a dull Tuesday into a wild escapade."

At that, Jeff's eyes lit with amusement. His smile deepened the faint laugh lines around his mouth. "He sounds like quite the character," he said, taking a small sip of coffee. "I like him already."

I chuckled, feeling relaxed. "Oh, he is. Truly. You have no idea. He's always traveling somewhere— Brazil one month, Greece the next—wherever the light is good, and his restless spirit leads him. He decided to take a vacation home to South Africa and visit his mother, and he started teasing me that I should join him. He joked that if he brought a gorgeous woman home, his mother might finally give up on her idea that he was gay."

I paused there to note Jeff's reaction. He arched a brow, a playful glimmer in his eyes. "And were you that 'gorgeous woman' he had in mind?" he teased gently.

"Apparently so," I replied with a grin. "At the time, it sounded ridiculous—I mean, I didn't have the money to be jetting off around the world, and my business was in a delicate stage. Running a modeling agency in Las Vegas is a constant balancing act. But Vimmi teased and teased. One day, for reasons I still can't fully explain, I got caught in his energy and asked my secretary to book me on the same flight. I thought maybe I'd scare him by showing him my ticket and announcing I was going home with him. It was to be a joke."

Jeff let out a genuine laugh that set my heart at ease. He leaned closer, arms still folded. "A bold plan," he said appreciatively.

"Yeah, well, it backfired a bit." I winced, recalling that moment of realization. "The secretary I had at the time was new—a pleasing person but not exactly well-versed in the intricacies of airfare regulations. She bought me a non-refundable, non-transferable ticket. So suddenly, I wasn't toying with the idea. I was staring at a confirmation email for a trip to Johannesburg that I either had to take or lose every penny I'd spent." My shoulders lifted in a helpless shrug. "In that split second, I went from half-joking to dead serious."

Jeff's grin widened, revealing a flicker of amusement and empathy. "That's quite the cosmic nudge," he remarked, drumming his fingertips lightly on the table. "I can see why you'd be torn, though. Joberg is not exactly around the corner."

I nodded, letting my gaze flicker around the vibrant café. The sun cast shimmering spots of light across the black-and-white tile floor, and the smell of freshly ground espresso woven with the faint aroma of spices drifted in from the street. "Torn is putting it lightly," I said. "My first thought was how to cancel, get my money back, or sell the ticket to someone else. But every time I tried, I hit a roadblock. The universe was gently refusing to let me wriggle out of this chance. It felt oddly like fate."

He raised his coffee cup to his lips, hiding a thoughtful smile. "So how do you get from that point—considering every way to wriggle out—to boarding the plane?"

I exhaled, remembering all the internal arguments I'd had in the days leading up to my flight. "I started thinking about why I was so resistant. Was it money? Was it fear? Was it the inertia of everyday life? For months, I'd been feeling stuck, like I was running on a treadmill at home. Get up, deal with clients, check off tasks, watch TV, go to bed. Rinse and repeat. I was missing something, a sense of real adventure, maybe. I used to be more spontaneous but lost that spirit."

"People get caught in their routines," Jeff agreed, nodding. "It's comfortable, predictable, safe—until it starts feeling stifling." His expression softened. "I know what it's like to want more than what's right in front of you."

That honest statement from him made my heart flutter. Without meaning to, I also found myself leaning in, drawn by the empathy in his voice. "Exactly," I said. "So, there I was with this ticket I was convinced I couldn't use. But something stopped me each time I picked up my phone to cancel. Finally, I asked myself: What if I... went? What if I saw it as a once-in-a-lifetime nudge instead of fighting it?"

His lips curved into an appreciative smile. "And you boarded the plane."

"And I boarded the plane," I echoed, laughing softly. "It still feels surreal. I barely slept. My mind was whirling with excitement one minute and raw panic the next. Then I landed, walked through customs, told my silly story to the officer, and found myself at a hotel in the city center—still waiting for it all to sink in."

Jeff set his cup down and regarded me for a long moment, the lines around his eyes crinkling as though he saw me in a new light. "People don't typically cross hemispheres on a whim," he observed, "but maybe more people should.

25

The world might be better if we acted on those adventurous impulses now and then."

It struck me then how comforting his presence was, how natural it felt to share my story in this open-air café on a Johannesburg street. The battered red umbrellas overhead rustled in a subtle breeze, sending flickering shadows dancing across our table. A swirl of language and color enveloped us: passersby speaking rapid-fire Zulu or softly accented English, clacking high heels against the pavement, and the squeal of a bus's brakes in the distance. For a moment, I allowed myself to pause, to soak in that swirl of city energy. It felt intoxicating.

"I'm glad I'm here too," I said earnestly. "Already, there's a vibe I can't quite explain. Everything seems alive here. Like the city itself has a pulse."

Jeff smiled, and for a second, the aura of politeness fell away, replaced by genuine fondness for his city. "It does," he murmured. "Johannesburg is complicated, and it's changing so fast. There's a mix of hardship and hope on every corner. It has a way of drawing people in, especially if they're looking for something new."

I looked around, following his gaze to a group of friends sharing a plate of pastries at a nearby table, to a street vendor stacking his displays of beaded bracelets and carved wooden figures, to the arching facade of an old building covered in vibrant street art. "I think I've been craving something exactly like this," I admitted, my voice dropping into something above a whisper. "A place that challenges me by being itself."

He chuckled softly. "I like that description— 'challenges me by being itself.' It's fitting. This city can be overwhelming, but it's also captivating. And you," he added, his voice gentling, "you seem like someone ready for a bit of overwhelm."

I laughed, warmth creeping into my cheeks. "No choice now, right?" I teased, though I felt a genuine stir of excitement inside me. "I'm here, and there's no going back.. at least not for a couple of weeks."

Jeff responded with a quiet grin, and a moment later, he reached across the small table and briefly touched my hand. His fingertips were warm against my skin, and that simple gesture—that tiny point of contact—grounded me in a way I hadn't expected. It was a fleeting touch, gone in seconds, yet it lingered in my mind.

"Well," he said, leaning back in his chair, "I am glad the universe conspired to bring you here. You never know what magic can happen when you listen to life's little signals instead of ignoring them."

I swallowed, smiling shyly. "Sometimes, I feel like I needed a big, neon sign to realize how much I craved a change."

He laughed then, the sound rich and genuine. "From the sound of it, you got one—the non-refundable ticket is as neon as it gets."

"True," I conceded, sipping my coffee. The robust flavor spread warmth through my chest, and

I wondered if I'd ever find coffee this good back home. "I wish I'd had the courage sooner. I might have missed so many experiences because I was too busy being practical."

A comfortable silence laced with unspoken understanding settled between us. In that lull, I noticed the angled sunlight reflecting off windows, the swirl of voices and car horns that was a steady undercurrent of life here. It was as though the world moved in slow motion for an instant, letting me savor the tactile reality of being far from home yet unexpectedly at ease.

"You know," Jeff said quietly, "I get it. I used to be the kind of person who always stuck to the plan, too. Like if I deviated, the world might spin off its axis. But life has a sense of humor."

My gaze flicked up. I wanted to learn more about him, this near-stranger who understood the call of adventure. "How so?" I prompted gently.

He shrugged, the gesture accompanied by a slight, thoughtful head tilt. "Let's say I had my sign once. Not quite a non-refundable ticket, but something close enough." His fingers drummed against the table again, a soft, rhythmic tapping. "I made a snap decision to move here years ago—left a country in turmoil and all that I had worked for. I left everything behind. My friends called me crazy. But at the time, I knew I had to do it."

On the Corner of Coetze and Klein

Something in his eyes told me he wasn't exaggerating. "And have you regretted it?" I asked softly.

His smile was slow, easy. "Not for a second. Hard as it was, I've come to believe that regret is worse than fear. Fear is natural—it keeps us sharp. But regret..." He shook his head, looking away for the briefest moment as if remembering something painful. "Regret can eat you up."

His words resonated in the space between us, a gentle reminder that life was short and full of forks in the road. "I think I'm only learning that," I murmured, and in my mind, I pictured the sum of all the years I'd spent on safe roads. "But better late than never, right?"

"Absolutely," he agreed. "You're here now, and that's all that matters."

I smiled, returning my attention to the swirl of the city. From somewhere down the block, a faint melody reached our ears—the strumming of a guitar accompanied by a soulful voice. Street performers, maybe. The sound fit seamlessly with the scene: the pastel-hued sunlight, the kaleidoscope of people, and the gentle clink of glassware on tabletops. Everything at that moment felt vibrant and alive, as though the city was weaving its music into our conversation.

After a moment, Jeff raised his coffee cup in a small salute. "So, here's to new adventures," he said, a grin tugging at one corner of his mouth.

I mirrored his action, lightly tapping my cup's rim to his before each took a sip. "To new adventures," I echoed. The phrase lingered in my throat, sweet and promising. The scent of cinnamon from the pastries behind the counter mingled with a nearby vendor's savory aroma of grilled meats. It enveloped us in a heady mixture that teased all the senses.

Suddenly aware of how at ease I felt, I caught Jeff studying me. Not in a predatory way, but with a soft, thoughtful curiosity, as if he were trying to piece together who I was beyond the impulsive traveler. I didn't find it unsettling. If anything, it was oddly flattering—like someone wanted to know what made me tick. "So," he said at last, "now that you've arrived, what's next?

"I've signed up for a city tour. I'm hoping to take a lot of photographs."

Jeff's eyes lit up. "The photo ops here are incredible, especially if you want to explore beyond the touristy stuff. And if you need any pointers on where to go or how to get there, let me know. I'm kind of a local guide for my friends who visit. I might not be a professional photographer, but I know my way around."

I couldn't help but smile at his offer. "I might take you up on that," I said softly. A warmth in his voice hinted he genuinely meant it, that this wasn't an empty gesture. "I'd love to see more than the obvious landmarks. Sometimes, you can find the best memories off the beaten path."

He nodded in agreement, and I sensed our easy camaraderie deepening. For a moment, I imagined the days ahead—stepping off the main roads, tasting local street food, hearing music in hidden venues, and capturing stolen moments through the camera lens. It felt electrifying. And somewhere in that tapestry of possibility, I imagined crossing paths with Jeff again—maybe showing him the silly souvenirs I'd picked up or letting him laugh at my attempts to pronounce local phrases.

"I'm curious," Jeff said after a beat, "how are you feeling about this now that you're here? That initial adrenaline rush must have been wild, but do you feel settled?"

I considered his question seriously. "In some ways, I'm still in that haze of jet lag and excitement. But there's a strange sense of belonging, too. Like, I know I'm an outsider—my accent, style, everything about me screams 'tourist.' But there's also this sense that I'm exactly where I'm meant to be, at least for now. I can't explain it better than that."

He reached out again, resting his palm lightly atop my hand in a gesture that felt comforting and reassuring. "That feeling," he said, his voice dipping quieter, "is what I love about travel. When you land in a place you've never been, and for reasons beyond logic, it feels like home—or a home you didn't know you needed. It's a rush."

A surge of gratitude welled up in me. I was grateful for his words, the city, and the random misadventures that had led me to this moment. "Exactly," I whispered. "I've always believed in signs but sometimes brushed them aside. Now, it's like the sign hit me over the head and said, 'Wake up, there's more to life than your office and your day planner.'"

Jeff chuckled. "Sometimes the universe does that. It's not always subtle when we've been ignoring the gentle nudges." He gave my hand a final squeeze and withdrew his touch, though the warmth remained even after his hand was gone. "I say embrace it. Let yourself experience everything this trip has to offer."

Another short silence unfurled, not awkward, but one that allowed me to breathe and check in with myself. The longer I looked at him, the more I realized how genuine this man was. In my usual routine, I rarely paused long enough to let real human connection in—especially with someone I'd only met. Yet here we were, bearing pieces of our lives like old friends.

"I will," I said, my voice soft but resolute. "No more letting fear talk me out of trying something new."

A flicker of approval lit up his eyes. "Good. Because if there's one thing you'll find in Johannesburg, it's something new—every day."

We both laughed then, a sound that folded seamlessly into the growing chorus: the slide of chairs on concrete, the hum of conversation as more people filtered in, and the distant echo of traffic.

"I could listen to you talk about this city for hours," I admitted. "Your passion is contagious."

He shrugged good-naturedly, but a hint of pride lingered in his grin. "We have our share of problems," he acknowledged, "but there's a heartbeat here that I've never found anywhere else. People are resilient and resourceful. And the cultures… it's this tapestry you can't describe until you see it yourself."

"Which I plan to," I replied, feeling that indescribable sense of possibility swirl through my veins. I glanced at my empty coffee cup, then back at Jeff. "Thank you for letting me ramble about my crazy story."

He chuckled. "You're not rambling. I asked, didn't I? And I find your story inspiring. It takes guts to do what you did—life forced your hand a little, sure, but you still had to follow through."

I blushed again, fiddling with my napkin. "I guess it's easier to see it as gutsy once you're sitting in a café in Johannesburg," I teased. "When I was back in Vegas, it felt like I was being reckless."

"Reckless can be good," he teased right back, reaching for his napkin as he contemplated ordering another drink. "Keeps life interesting."

A gentle breeze swept through the outdoor seating area, fluttering the edges of the umbrellas and bringing a cool reprieve from the heat. The laughter of a nearby table drifted toward us, and I caught snippets of conversation—someone exclaiming over a dish they'd tried, another describing a crazy day at work. It felt so real, so ordinary in the best possible way.

I reflected on how, back home, I'd often sit in the same spot at my usual café, day after day, never really noticing the conversation around me. Here, I felt hyper-aware of every detail: the architecture, the swirl of languages, the curious glances of strangers. Travel amplifies the senses, as though you need to absorb every new stimulus so you won't forget it once you're gone.

Jeff caught my slight pause, his expression turning inquisitive. "Penny for your thoughts?" he asked.

I offered a slight shrug, a half-smile tugging at my lips. " I've already seen more and felt more in one morning here than in months back home. It's like my senses are awake for the first time in forever."

He nodded thoughtfully. "That's the beauty of being out of your comfort zone—everything becomes sharper. You pay attention. You soak it all in."

"And you meet interesting people," I added softly, meeting his gaze. It was a bit bolder than I intended, but it felt true.

"And that," I thought to myself, "is exactly why people travel—to find moments that break the usual rhythm of life, that let you see something or meet someone you never expected."

Jeff rose to his feet, and I took that as my cue to do the same. We both thanked the waiter, stepping away from the table. The street beyond the café seemed a little less daunting now, suffused with the glow of a waning sun. Cars passed by steadily, and shadows grew longer across the pavement.

He turned to me, an easy, open smile on his face. "Can I drive you back to your hotel?"

"Thank you, no," I replied. "But you can walk me back if you would like,"

His eyes lingered on mine for a heartbeat longer. "I can do that," he said with a quiet sincerity. "Johannesburg can be big and overwhelming, but it can also be magical. I hope you see that side of it."

Part of me wanted to stroll aimlessly, letting the city unfold around me. Another part longed to head back to the hotel. But my curiosity won out, propelled by the lingering warmth of that unexpected invitation from a stranger named Jeff Holman. My feet began to move, camera in hand, scanning for the next detail, the next moment worth capturing.

And so, at the corner of Coetze and Klein—where I'd nearly clutched my camera bag in panic at a stranger's tap—I found something else entirely: the first glimmer of belonging in a city I barely knew. That simple gesture, that brief introduction, became the start of a story I never could have scripted. In the glow of that afternoon sun, beneath red umbrellas and the hum of traffic, my journey in Johannesburg began in earnest, leaving me both exhilarated and a little unsure but strangely confident that I was exactly where I needed to be.

That, quite simply, was how I met Jeff Holman: divorced, a few years older than me, originally from Rhodesia, and wholly determined to speak to the American woman who had landed in Johannesburg less than twenty-four hours prior. I had no inkling then of the twists and turns to come—only the sense that the city had opened itself, only a crack, to let me glimpse a new chapter of my life waiting to unfold.

With one last look at the cheerful red umbrellas behind me, I took my first step away from the café. Each footfall on the pavement felt like a promise to myself—a vow to keep embracing the unfamiliar and trusting the nudges of fate. Because sometimes, the best things happen when we're brave—or foolish—enough to answer adventure's call.

For a brief moment, we let the quiet linger. The city noise was still there—always there—but in the golden light of the afternoon, it felt muffled as if the cafés, cars, and crowds had formed a comforting soundtrack rather than an assault on the senses. With some wonder, I realized that I didn't feel rushed anymore. My typical travel anxiety—where to go next, what to see, how to stay safe—had dimmed into the background. Here, on the terrace of a small café at the corner of Coetze and Klein, I felt oddly rooted, as though this fleeting moment was all I needed.

Chapter 3
An Unexpected Guide

He offered to show me around Johannesburg, but I politely declined, explaining that I'd already booked a couple of tours for the upcoming days—museum visits, a guided excursion through Soweto, and a 3-day trip to the Kruger National Park. I didn't want him to feel like he had to reinvent the wheel for me. But Jeff only smiled, undaunted, and said, "Then I'll take you up on that walk back to the hotel. "No strings attached," he said with an easy shrug, "just two travelers sharing conversation."

On the surface, it felt harmless—a short stroll, fifteen minutes at most. I almost backed out, thinking about how I'd hardly known this man for more than a couple of hours, but something in his demeanor felt honest and transparent. I found myself nodding, curiosity getting the better of me. "Sure," I said. "Let's walk."

What began as a seemingly brief walk quickly became a leisurely, winding journey that lasted nearly two hours. Our path took us along broad avenues lined with tall buildings and bustling shops before detouring down narrow, often overlooked side streets. Jeff seemed to know every hidden corner of Johannesburg, pointing out little details that even some locals might miss. He stopped at an alleyway where a faded brick wall displayed an intricate mural—a burst of blue and orange that told a story of struggle and triumph. As we paused there, Jeff explained that the local artist had once been a political activist, using art to voice dissent and inspire hope.

I was fascinated by Johannesburg's blend of contrasting styles: old colonial-era buildings with their intricate facades and wrought-iron balconies stood side by side with sleek, modern structures wrapped in tinted glass. It was as if the city was in a constant state of reinvention, holding tightly to fragments of its storied past while simultaneously pushing toward a vibrant future. The streets themselves hummed with life; hawkers called out to us, their tables bursting with textiles in kaleidoscopic patterns—crimson, cobalt, vivid yellows—while others showcased fresh fruits, sizzling street food, or bins of pungent spices that filled the air with an intoxicating mix of aromas.

Jeff navigated this frenetic environment with a casual confidence that soon put me at ease. Occasionally, he'd pause to greet someone—a vendor he'd shared a laugh with over his lunch break or a security guard stationed at the door of an office tower. His warm, genuine interactions reminded me that cities are more than just their buildings and roads; they're vibrant tapestries woven from countless human connections.

At one point, we stopped at a stall showcasing bright beadwork: necklaces, bracelets, and keychains, all shimmering with intricate patterns. Various leather goods hung from weathered wooden posts, and the rich scent of cured hides drifted in the air. The vendor—a petite woman sporting a cobalt headscarf—flashed me a friendly smile, and I couldn't help but notice the craftsmanship. As I turned a brightly beaded bracelet over in my hands, Jeff leaned in and explained a few everyday phrases in Zulu and Afrikaans, his voice low and encouraging. "Try saying 'ngiyabonga,'" he said softly, his eyes sparkling with delight as he slowly pronounced it for me. I stumbled over the syllables, eliciting a hearty laugh from him. "Not bad at all," he teased gently, repeating the phrase until I managed to get closer to the proper intonation. At that moment, I felt the electric thrill of learning something entirely new, a small yet significant step into the heart of Johannesburg.

As we left the stall—my pockets now a little heavier with two irresistible bracelets—I couldn't help but notice how the light was changing. The sun was slipping lower in the sky, bathing the streets in a warm, golden glow that seemed to make every

41

color richer and every sound crisper. The laughter of children playing on the sidewalks blended seamlessly with the multilingual chatter that floated through the air, and the constant murmur of traffic was like the city's heartbeat.

Our conversation flowed easily as we walked. Jeff talked about his love for the city, his tone both nostalgic and optimistic. "You know," he said, glancing at a row of old buildings with peeling paint and ornate details, "each brick here has a story. Some carry memories of happier times, and others bear scars of hardship. But that makes Johannesburg so alive—it's always evolving." I listened, captivated by his words and how he saw beauty in every crack and crevice. His enthusiasm was infectious, and I found myself sharing bits about my journey, the twists and turns that had led me here. It was surprising how quickly trust began to build between us, even as the unfamiliar city sprawled out like a puzzle waiting to be solved.

Eventually, our stroll brought us to a quieter part of the city. We ambled along streets flanked by small cafés and boutique stores, where the buzz of the metropolis softened into a more intimate hum. The setting sun had now fully embraced the horizon, casting long, languid shadows and painting the sky in hues of lavender and peach. In these moments, Johannesburg felt almost like a secret garden hidden within the urban sprawl, where time slowed down enough to appreciate every subtle detail.

On the Corner of Coetze and Klein

Reaching the Landrost Hotel, I marveled at the building's imposing façade. The lobby was undeniably grand: vast marble floors gleamed under the light of ornate chandeliers, and tall, stately potted palms stood like silent guardians at the edges of the spacious room. I couldn't help but feel a little out of place amid such luxury. Yet, with Jeff's reassuring presence by my side, that self-consciousness quickly melted away.

We lingered in the lobby as I fished for my room key, the cool air-conditioning providing a welcome respite from the lingering heat of the late afternoon. I contemplated how best to end our unexpected excursion—perhaps a simple goodbye with a promise to reconnect later—but before I could voice my thoughts, Jeff's eyes roamed the elegant space before settling back on me with a gentle smile.

"Are you hungry?" he asked in a casual and hopeful tone. "How about dinner?"

A mix of emotions fluttered through me— surprise, intrigue, and a cautious wariness. I didn't know him well enough yet, and the familiar warnings about trusting strangers in foreign lands whispered in the back of my mind. But as I looked into his warm eyes, I sensed a sincerity that dispelled any lingering doubts. He wasn't trying to corner or pressure me; he simply invited me to continue sharing the evening.

After a brief moment of deliberation, I nodded. "Sure," I said cautiously, "but let's keep it here in the hotel dining room."

His face lit up as if I'd just handed him a golden ticket. "Of course," he said with a lopsided grin that instantly made me feel like I'd made the right choice. "I'd be honored."

I mirrored his grin, a small weight of relief settling over me. It was remarkable how one spontaneous decision—a simple acceptance of a stranger's company—had already transformed my day. The morning, which had begun with the uncertainty of a lone traveler in a vast, unfamiliar city, had unfolded into a series of delightful surprises, each more unexpected than the last.

As we made our way toward the hotel dining room, the soft clack of our footsteps echoed off the marble floor. The restaurant's entrance, framed by etched glass panels that hinted at an elegant interior, beckoned us inside. The atmosphere shifted as we entered: subdued lighting, soft murmurs of conversation, and the distant clinking of cutlery created an ambiance of refined comfort. A courteous host greeted us and led us to a quiet corner table, its surface polished to a high shine and adorned with a single, flickering candle.

We settled into a quiet corner of the dining room where the gentle hum of conversation from nearby tables provided a soothing backdrop. Every so often, the soft clink of silverware or the muted chime of glasses punctuated the air as if the restaurant itself were participating in our unfolding dialogue. Our waiter appeared promptly, dressed in a crisp white shirt and tailored black waistcoat. He set down sleek leather-bound menus with quiet professionalism and poured water into our delicate goblets. Before long, he recommended a South African Cabernet Sauvignon—a full-bodied wine with hints of blackberry and spice that promised to complement the evening's fare perfectly.

Jeff didn't hesitate. He ordered a glass immediately, his practiced hand swirling and sniffing the wine as if it were an art form. Watching him, I couldn't help but see him in a new light. The confident yet thoughtful way he handled even the most minor details hinted at a life of experience, of both hardships overcome and quiet victories savored. His manner had an unmistakable gravity—a calm resilience gained from unpredictable challenges.

As we waited for our meals, conversation flowed as quickly as the wine. The low lighting and the sumptuous surroundings gave the entire experience an almost cinematic quality. I found myself leaning in, drawn by the elegant space's physical comfort and our dialogue's unexpected intimacy.

"Tell me," I began tentatively, "what's your story, Jeff? How did you end up in Johannesburg doing what you do?"

He smiled a slow, slightly off-center expression that suggested both amusement and the weight of many memories. "I suppose it all started back in Rhodesia," he said, swirling his wine as he recalled his past. "I grew up where well-tended gardens and manicured lawns were the norm—a promise of endless prosperity, or so it seemed. But when political tensions escalated, let's say we were forced to leave. I even call it a sort of 'communist takeover' in retrospect." His tone was reflective, not bitter—a quiet acceptance of fate's unpredictable turns.

He leaned back, his gaze momentarily drifting toward the softly lit window as if searching for the ghosts of his former life. "Moving to South Africa wasn't just a change of scenery—it was the abrupt end of one grand chapter and the uncertain start of another. I arrived in Johannesburg with nothing but a suitcase full of immaculate suits and a head full of ambition. For a while, I managed to carve out a life among the influential, mingling with business people and sipping fine champagne at glittering soirées. But amid all that opulence, there was an undercurrent of loneliness, a shadow I couldn't quite shake off." He paused, then gave a playful wink. "Maybe that's one reason I wasn't afraid to chase you down on the street earlier—I've learned to seize opportunities before they pass me by."

His words caught me off guard, and I felt a subtle flutter in my stomach. It wasn't crude or presumptuous; instead, it was an open admission wrapped in playful charm. I found myself smiling in return, the warmth in his eyes inviting me to share his story. "It sounds like you've had quite a journey," I replied softly, stirring my wine absentmindedly as I processed his confession.

Jeff's eyes crinkled with a mixture of nostalgia and resilience. "We lose almost everything in those transitions," he continued. "But starting over teaches you resilience, the strength that doesn't come from avoiding pain but rising above it. I've learned that every loss carries its lesson—even if it means leaving behind a life I once thought I'd built."

Our conversation meandered as gracefully as the wine's lingering finish. Between bites of our carefully chosen dishes—succulent cuts of beef for him and a delicately spiced seafood dish for me—we traded stories of our contrasting worlds. Jeff spoke of his career importing raw materials from neighboring countries and of long journeys between South Africa, Zimbabwe, and Mozambique, where he negotiated deals that often went unnoticed by the casual observer. His voice was animated as he recalled the intricacies of those negotiations and the quiet hustle behind Africa's economic engine that tourists rarely saw.

At one point, as we shared a particularly hearty laugh over a mishap story during one of his previous tours, I noticed a subtle shift in his tone. He leaned in slightly, his eyes glinting with a mix of mischief and something else—something I couldn't quite place. "There's so much more to Johannesburg than what you see on the surface," he confided softly.

"Every corner has a secret, every smile a hidden story." His words hung in the air like a promise of undiscovered adventures, and I found myself hanging on to every syllable.

In contrast, I recounted my life in Las Vegas—a city of neon lights and perpetual motion. "You wouldn't believe it," I said, laughing as I described the endless nights filled with the buzz of slot machines and the ceaseless parade of wide-eyed tourists. "Sometimes it feels like I'm a spectator in my own life, watching the spectacle unfold from behind a shimmering veil." Jeff listened intently, his eyes never leaving mine, occasionally leaning in to ask a thoughtful follow-up question that made me feel heard in a rare and unexpectedly profound way.

The conversation shifted seamlessly from the grand narratives of cities and economies to the subtle personal experiences that defined us. Jeff recounted a story from his time in Europe, where he'd once gotten hopelessly lost in the winding backstreets of Lisbon. "I ended up in a little fado bar," he recalled with a chuckle, his eyes lighting up as he remembered the haunting music and the spontaneous camaraderie of strangers who welcomed him as though he were an old friend. The memory was so vivid that for a moment, I could almost hear the melancholic strains of the Portuguese ballads filling the space between us.

On the Corner of Coetze and Klein

I, in turn, admitted the surprising loneliness that sometimes gripped me in Las Vegas—a loneliness that belied the city's relentless energy. "It's strange," I mused, "to be surrounded by millions yet feel so isolated. There's always a crowd, always noise, but sometimes it's like the city never really sees you." Jeff nodded in agreement, his gaze thoughtful as he sipped his wine, acknowledging that big cities, no matter how vibrant, often had a way of making you feel small.

Dinner continued with an ease that made the hours slip by unnoticed. The conversation turned to art, history, and the inevitable blending of cultures that defined the city. I shared my impressions of the day—the colors, the sounds, and the seemingly endless surprises—and Jeff listened with an intensity that made me feel like my words mattered. It was as if, at that moment, we were co-authors of a shared narrative, each of us contributing to the story of Johannesburg in our unique way.

As dessert arrived—a plate of tiny, artfully arranged pastries on gleaming white porcelain—I was more captivated by the conversation than the food itself. The delicate flavors of the sweets, a perfect counterpoint to the robust meal we'd enjoyed, provided a fitting punctuation to the rich tapestry of our dialogue. In those quiet moments, the world outside the restaurant seemed to fade away, leaving only the soft murmur of our voices and the unspoken understanding that this was a night of discoveries—not of the city, but of ourselves.

Then, the bill was discreetly placed on the table as if on cue. I instinctively reached for my purse, ready to insist on splitting the check. But before I could protest, Jeff gently rested his hand over mine, his touch warm and reassuring. "Please," he said, his tone both decisive and tender. "Let me take care of this."

His calm decisiveness, so old-fashioned and sincere, disarmed me completely. In that small gesture, I saw a reflection of his character—a man who, despite life's uncertainties, still believed in chivalry and the simple acts of kindness that connect us. I smiled and nodded, feeling both grateful and a little wistful as he signed the slip with a flourish, handing it back to the waiter with a courteous nod.

After dinner, we left the dining room and began our stroll back through the hotel's grand lobby. The marble floor gleamed under the light of ornate chandeliers, and large mirrors reflected the delicate glow of wall sconces, amplifying the sense of timeless elegance that seemed to envelop the space. Guests drifted by in quiet conversation while uniformly attired staff moved gracefully about, attending to each guest with a practiced, almost ritualistic precision.

Jeff pressed the call button at the elevator and then turned to me with a gentle, lingering smile. "I'll call you," he said softly as the elevator doors slid open, his voice imbued with a promise rather than a simple goodbye. For a moment, our eyes met—a silent exchange filled with all the unspoken implications of the evening. I thanked him for dinner, trembling slightly with excitement and an inexplicable longing.

Once inside my room, I found myself restless on the plush bed, the city lights flickering through the gap in the curtains. The memories of our dinner— his candid confessions, the artful way he recounted his past, and the ease with which we shared our lives—played over in my mind like the opening notes of a long-awaited song. Despite the promise of tomorrow's tours and activities, I sensed that my time in Johannesburg was already irrevocably colored by his presence. There was a depth to him that hinted at further stories, and I couldn't shake the anticipation of discovering what lay beneath the surface.

I lay there, replaying every word, every smile, and every pause that had filled the space between us during dinner. The rich tapestry of our conversation seemed to echo in the room's quiet—a blend of history, personal triumphs and losses, and the bittersweet flavor of second chances. The hotel room felt less like a temporary refuge and more like a stage set for the next chapter of a story I was only beginning to understand.

As I drifted between wakefulness and sleep, my thoughts returned to Jeff's parting words at the elevator. There was something tender yet determined in how he'd said he'd call me—a quiet promise that our encounter was not merely a fleeting moment but the start of something more profound. Even now, as the city's nocturnal hum seeped through the window and mingled with my quiet introspection, I felt that the evening had planted seeds of change deep within me.

The more I thought about it, the more I realized that tonight wasn't only about an elegant dinner in a grand old hotel. It was about the unanticipated intersections of lives—how a chance meeting on a bustling Johannesburg street could lead to an exchange of stories, vulnerabilities, and, perhaps, dreams. Jeff's gentle insistence on seizing opportunities resonated with me, challenging the boundaries of my cautious existence.

I wondered about the future, about the possibilities that tomorrow might bring. In Johannesburg—a city of contrasts, where history and modernity coexisted in an ever-evolving dance— each moment carried the potential for discovery. As I lay there, the soft rhythm of my heartbeat blending with the distant sounds of the city, I couldn't help but feel that my journey was taking on an entirely new meaning.

Maybe, just maybe, Jeff's presence was a sign—a subtle invitation to embrace the unexpected, to let down my guard, and to allow the city, with all its hidden gems and whispered secrets, to reveal itself in ways I'd never imagined. The memory of his warm eyes and the sincere cadence of his voice lingered like a gentle refrain, urging me to look beyond the familiar and into life's vast, unfolding landscape.

And so, with the night deepening around me and the promise of dawn waiting beyond the horizon, I closed my eyes, determined to let the quiet anticipation guide me into dreams filled with the hope of new beginnings. Little did I know that this was only the prologue to a story that would continue to unravel, full of joyful and bittersweet discoveries—a story that, like the city itself, was as unpredictable as it was mesmerizing.

Chapter 4
City Exploration

The following morning, South African sunshine burst through the curtains of my hotel room like a promise. Even though I'd stayed up late the previous night, caught in the pleasant haze of conversation with Jeff, I woke with a surprising burst of energy. Today marked the start of my organized tours—a chance to explore Johannesburg's layered history and vibrant present. As I gathered my things, I couldn't help but feel that the day held countless possibilities.

I joined a small group of fellow travelers in the bustling hotel lobby. The mix was as diverse as it was exciting: a few travelers from England, a couple from Australia, and others from various parts of Asia, all united by our shared curiosity about this extraordinary country. There was an easy camaraderie in our huddled formation as we exchanged brief introductions and friendly banter. One fellow traveler from Australia, a sunburned chap with a quick laugh, remarked, "I've heard Johannesburg is like a living museum—where every corner has a story to tell." His words resonated with the hopeful excitement buzzing around us.

Soon enough, we climbed aboard a tour bus that was as colorful and spirited as the city itself. I sat by a window, eager to watch Johannesburg's sprawling skyline come into view. As the bus pulled away, I marveled at the architectural patchwork outside: remnants of colonial edifices, sleek glass-fronted high-rises, and art deco landmarks coexisted with bold, modern street art that splashed vibrant murals onto otherwise drab walls. Every face on the bus lit up as we wound through the city's busy streets, and even the most seasoned travelers couldn't hide their amazement at the ever-changing scenery.

Our guide for the day, a jovial man named Abner, introduced himself with a lilting accent that made even the driest historical facts sound poetic. "Welcome, my friends," he greeted us with a broad smile, his eyes twinkling with mischief and pride. "Today, we'll journey through the soul of Johannesburg—from the echoes of the gold rush to the vibrant heartbeat of its modern culture." His enthusiasm was contagious, and soon, we were all leaning in as he recounted the city's explosive growth fueled by the gold rush of the late 19th century. He described how fortunes were made and lost beneath the glare of the African sun and how the promise of gold transformed a dusty outpost into a bustling metropolis.

On the Corner of Coetze and Klein

Our first stop was the Apartheid Museum. Stepping into the solemn, darkened halls, the weight of history pressed in on us. I noticed tears glistening in the eyes of a few fellow travelers, and I found myself pausing in silence, absorbing the raw emotions conveyed through photographs, artifacts, and interactive exhibits. One visitor, a middle-aged woman from England, whispered to her friend, "It's like walking through the very soul of sorrow and resilience." Abner's gentle narration helped us navigate the painful chapters of history, making it clear that while the past was marred by injustice, it also bore witness to a people's unyielding determination to overcome adversity.

Leaving the museum, Abner shifted the day's tone by taking us to a lively cultural center. There, we watched an impromptu performance by African dancers whose vibrant energy lit up the room. Their costumes—intricately beaded skirts, feathered headpieces, and jangling anklets—moved with a rhythmic abandon that seemed to channel the very spirit of Africa. I found myself clapping along, mesmerized by the dancers' fluid grace. Abner leaned between the drums' beats and the swish of colorful fabrics and explained, "These dances are not only art; they're stories passed down through generations, a language of joy and pain all at once." The performance sparked a flurry of whispered discussions among the group. One Asian traveler mentioned, "I've never seen movement tell a story

so beautifully. It's as if every step is a memory."
I couldn't agree more—the experience was
mesmerizing and profoundly moving.

Our next stop was a bustling local market that
seemed to capture the essence of Johannesburg. The
air was alive with scents that ranged from the smoky
aroma of freshly grilled meat to the rich, inviting
perfume of roasted coffee beans and even the
piquant tang of exotic spices. I wandered between
stalls, my camera clicking away as I captured candid
photos of stall owners beaming with pride, children
darting between market aisles, and local vendors
engaged in animated bargaining. I struck up a brief
conversation with a friendly woman selling woven
textiles. "Each of these fabrics tells a story," she said
in accented English, gently running her hand over a
vibrantly patterned cloth. "They are made by hands
that have seen both hardship and joy." Her words
lingered in my mind as I moved on, a small but
poignant reminder of the personal histories woven
into the everyday fabric of life.

But the true highlight of the day awaited us at
a historic gold mine—a tangible connection to the
very element that put Johannesburg on the map.
After a safety briefing and donning hard hats, we
descended into the cool, shadowed tunnels. The air
was thick with the earthy scent of damp stone, and
the echo of our footsteps on the rough floor stirred
my imagination. I could almost picture the miners
of old, chipping away in near-darkness, their faces

lit only by the faint glow of lanterns, all in pursuit of that elusive treasure. Our guide's deep voice explained the meticulous process of extracting gold from the raw, unforgiving rock, and I held my breath in awe.

Once our tour of the mine ended, we tried our hand at panning for gold in a shallow, man-made creek. The process was simple yet hypnotic—swirl the water in your pan, carefully sift out the dirt, and hope to catch a glimpse of shimmering flecks. More often than not, my pan filled with nothing more than muddy silt and gravel. Yet, when a few specks of gold caught the light, I couldn't help but let out a delighted laugh. "Look, I struck it rich!" I exclaimed, half in jest. A nearby traveler, a cheerful chap from Australia, teased, "Better buy us all a drink then!" Our laughter mingled with the gentle gurgle of the creek, and for a moment, the simple joy of the experience made the day feel almost magical.

The bus rumbled back toward central Johannesburg as the sun descended slowly. The window beside me framed a breathtaking canvas—the sky was a riot of oranges, pinks, and deep purples, each color reflecting off the city's skyline. I exchanged impressions with my new friends, each of us animatedly recalling our favorite moments of the day. One traveler from England remarked, "I never imagined that history could be so tangible, so right here beneath our feet." I nodded in agreement, feeling that the day had opened a window onto Johannesburg's past and its resilient spirit.

Pulling up to the Landrost Hotel in the early evening, I gathered my daypack and stepped off the bus, already feeling the pleasant ache of a well-done day. I planned to head to my room for a quick rest before dinner—only fate had other plans. As I approached the hotel entrance, I noticed a tall, familiar figure leaning casually against a lamppost near the curb. The soft glow from the hotel's facade illuminated Jeff's broad shoulders and relaxed stance, and my pulse fluttered in greeting.

"Hi," I said with a bright smile, casually slinging my bag over one shoulder. "What are you doing here?"

Jeff stepped forward, his warm smile lighting up his eyes. "I've come to make sure you get a good dinner," he replied, his tone as straightforward as it was sincere.

I couldn't help laughing, the unexpectedness of his appearance mingling with the pleasant buzz of the day. "Dinner, you say? Well, I could use it—I didn't realize how hungry I was until now." His easy charm and unassuming presence made it impossible not to be drawn into the moment.

Within minutes, we walked down a lively avenue, the cool evening air wrapping around us as we strolled toward a cozy bistro Jeff recommended. Tucked beside a row of eclectic shops, the bistro's modest sign read "Local Fare & Fine Wines," promising a taste of authentic South African comfort. As we stepped inside, the gentle glow of hanging lamps bathed the rustic wooden tables in a warm, inviting light. The air was rich with the aroma of grilled spices and hearty stews, and my stomach growled in anticipation.

We settled at a table near a window overlooking the soft, flickering city lights. The menu was a veritable feast for the senses—South African favorites abounded: biltong platters, bobotie, boerewors, and pap served with a tangy, rich tomato relish. Pap is very similar to what we in America call grits. We opted for grilled boerewors, thick and savory sausages spiced to perfection, paired with pap that was as comforting as filling. The meal was what I needed after a day of adventures—each bite a blend of rustic tradition and modern vibrancy.

Over dinner, our conversation flowed effortlessly. I recounted the thrill of the gold mine tour and the simple, childlike joy of panning for gold. "When I saw those little flecks sparkle in my pan, I felt like a kid discovering treasure for the first time," I said, laughing as I remembered the moment. Jeff listened with rapt attention, nodding and chuckling at the right moments. "That's exactly the kind of excitement you need to keep life interesting," he replied, his tone light yet thoughtful.

Then, as the conversation naturally shifted, Jeff began to share his own stories. He spoke of his childhood, growing up in Rhodesia's vast, open grasslands—long before it was renamed Zimbabwe. "I remember," he said softly, swirling his drink as if it held memories, "when storms would roll in across the plains, turning the sky a deep, dramatic purple. Lightning would dance on the horizon, and the scent of wet dust mingled with the promise of new beginnings." His voice carried the nostalgia of lost times and the wisdom of lessons learned. "Those storms were both beautiful and frightening. They taught me to cherish every calm moment."

His candor was captivating. Between bites of our flavorful meal, he told me about the upheavals that forced his family to leave behind the land they loved. "It's something you never forget," he murmured, eyes downcast for a moment, "but it also makes you value every small blessing." His words had a quiet strength—a resilience that had carried him through personal and historical storms. I found myself sharing a piece of my own story in the relentless neon buzz of Las Vegas. Jeff's empathetic gaze told me he understood; his experiences had forged him into someone who appreciated the beauty of genuine human connection.

We lingered over our meal, savoring the delicious flavors and the rare ease of genuine conversation. I noticed how the night deepened outside the bistro's window; the city's neon glow softened by the encroaching dark, yet the warmth inside made it all feel timeless. The clinking of cutlery and soft background music created a cocoon of intimacy, making every word seem personal and profound.

After finishing our meal—empty plates a silent testament to a shared enjoyment—we stepped out into the crisp night air. The streets were quieter now, the earlier bustle giving way to the gentle murmur of late-night revelers and the distant hum of traffic. As we strolled back to the Landrost Hotel under the glow of streetlights, our conversation turned to lighter topics: funny childhood mishaps, humorous cultural misunderstandings, and even our favorite foods. It was a delightful back-and-forth, filled with laughter and moments of comfortable silence, punctuating the newfound connection that had grown between us.

Back in the gleaming hotel lobby, the evening's gentle enchantment lingered. Jeff paused momentarily, deciding whether to extend our conversation or let the night close gently. Instead of an awkward goodbye, he smiled—a smile that carried a promise of future encounters. "Thank you for sharing this evening with me," he said quietly, his tone both sincere and hopeful. "I'd love to catch up again soon." As we approached the elevator, his words made my heart flutter with anticipation.

Once in my room, I sat on the edge of the plush bed, peeling off my shoes and placing the day's souvenirs—small tokens and mementos collected during the tour—on the dresser. The city's soft hum outside and the quiet tick of the bedside

63

clock provided a reflective soundtrack to the night. I replayed every moment: the raw emotions in the museum, the vibrant energy of the dance performance, the simple joy of panning for gold, and now, the warm, genuine connection with Jeff. Only two days earlier, I'd arrived as a wary traveler, unsure how to navigate this complex city. Now, I felt as though Johannesburg was beginning to reveal itself—not as a destination, but as a place where stories intertwined and new friendships bloomed.

I glanced at the clock on the bedside table, realizing I'd barely looked at it since the tour ended. Hours had slipped through my fingers like the shimmering grains of a sandy hourglass, yet I felt more alive than ever.

Lying there in the gentle embrace of night, I realized that the day had been a series of small, unexpected adventures. Each encounter, each shared laugh, and every story had added another layer to my understanding of this place. The vibrant chaos of Johannesburg had been balanced by our moments of quiet introspection and intimate conversation. And amid all this, Jeff had emerged as more than a fleeting companion—he had become a symbol of the city's unpredictable magic, a reminder that sometimes the most profound connections are forged in the unlikeliest circumstances.

I glanced again at the clock and the window, where the city lights shimmered like distant stars. As I settled into sleep, my thoughts danced between the promise of tomorrow's adventures and the lingering warmth of tonight's memories. In the back of my mind, I knew that my journey in Johannesburg was only beginning and that each day would unveil new layers of history, culture, and friendship.

As the night deepened, I drifted into sleep with a soft smile, feeling the gentle echo of Jeff's voice and the lively chatter of my new friends from the tour. It was a night of reflections and quiet hopes. This night promised that in Johannesburg, every moment was an opportunity for discovery, and every friendship, no matter how brief, could leave an indelible mark on the heart.

In that peaceful solitude, with the memories of the day swirling in my mind like the rich hues of a sunset over the city, I made a silent promise to myself: to remain open to every new experience, to savor each unexpected encounter, and to let the rhythm of Johannesburg guide me through both its bustling streets and its quiet, hidden corners. And in that promise lay the anticipation of countless adventures yet to come—a promise that the magic of this city was as boundless as the friendships it inspired.

Chapter 5
Into the Wild

The following day arrived in a flurry of excitement. Even the bustling lobby of the Landrost Hotel buzzed with anticipation as I slung my overnight bag over my shoulder and hurried to join the waiting bus. I'd signed up for a three-day tour of Kruger National Park—a dream adventure I'd fantasized about ever since I realized I was making the trip due to that non-refundable flight to South Africa. Somehow, my earlier adventures in Johannesburg had only intensified my eagerness to see the country's famed wildlife up close.

The Journey Begins

I boarded a small, comfortably appointed bus alongside seven other travelers—a delightfully eclectic mix of wanderers from around the globe. There was Lucy and Mark, a young couple from London whose eyes sparkled with excitement as they recounted their story of saving for this very trip since their engagement. Across the aisle, Ren and Carla from Sydney exchanged mischievous glances and whispered plans about "bagging a photo of the Big Five." And then there were three solo adventurers like me: Saeed from Dubai, meticulously adjusting his wide-brimmed hat; Akiko from Tokyo, whose quiet smile promised endless stories; and Mateo from Chile, scribbling notes in a little weathered journal.

As the bus rumbled away from Johannesburg, our conversation bubbled with enthusiasm. We swapped travel tips and wild expectations: "I can't wait to see a lion's mane up close," someone said, while another declared, "Imagine spotting a cheetah sprinting across the savanna!" I found myself laughing and nodding along, wholly immersed in the camaraderie of kindred spirits. I wasn't sure whether or not there was a savanna in this part of South Africa.

Outside, the cityscape slowly yielded to expansive highways flanked by farmlands. As we ventured further out, the scenery shifted subtly—a mosaic of low, scrubby trees and golden grasses that stretched like a living carpet under the endless African sky. Every roadside sign, every glimpse of a small market, felt like a snapshot of a world far removed from our everyday lives. As I sat by the window, I captured the rustic charm on my camera, and the conversation turned into a delightful back-and-forth about the hidden treasures of rural South Africa.

Arriving at the Heart of the Wild

By midday, the bus pulled up to the grand entrance gate of Kruger National Park. A massive, weathered sign welcomed us, and a few curious baboons perched on a nearby fence. They watched us with mischievous eyes, almost daring us to enter their domain. Our guide, Martin—a sprightly South African with a twinkle in his eye and a voice that seemed to carry the very rhythm of the bush—climbed aboard. "Remember, folks," he joked as he gestured at our bags, "keep your arms and belongings inside the bus, or these cheeky baboons might help themselves to a souvenir!" His playful tone set the stage for an adventure where nature held the power.

The bus wound its way deeper into the park, and every turn revealed yet another stunning vignette of the African wilderness. Soon, we were treating our eyes to a parade of animals in their natural habitat. Our first encounter was with a group of zebras grazing gracefully amidst the dry grass—a surreal sight against the dusty, sunlit backdrop. I couldn't help but let out a slight, delighted squeal as my heart soared at the simple, breathtaking reality: this was real. I was here, surrounded by nature's raw beauty.

Judi Moreo

Settling Into Our Rondavels

After a scenic drive that felt like a prelude to a symphony of wildlife, the bus eventually rolled into a fenced camp area. Clustered together were several charming round huts with thatched roofs—rondavels. With its circular design, sturdy walls, and carefully woven straw roof, each rondavel exuded a rustic yet welcoming vibe. Stepping inside one of these humble abodes was like entering a cool, breezy haven carved out of the bush, where the natural airflow worked its magic in the heat of the day.

I shared a cozy little rondavel with Akiko. The interior was simple, with smooth, polished wooden floors and walls that told tales of generations past. Akiko practically danced to the window, throwing the curtains wide open to reveal a view that took my breath away—a small waterhole glimmered in the distance, mirroring the vast, endless horizon. There, the bushveld stretched out in all its majesty: acacia trees punctuating the landscape, dusty paths winding through the tall grasses, and the sky painted in brilliant blues and soft whites. "It's like living in a postcard," Akiko whispered, and I couldn't agree more.

Before long, we had barely unpacked when Martin's friendly voice called us to the main reception. We were to meet him for our first late-afternoon game drive. Emerging from our rondavels,

On the Corner of Coetze and Klein

we caught sight of Lucy and Mark, who looked like they had stepped off the set of a safari fashion shoot—khaki shirts, matching hats, and binoculars dangling stylishly around their necks. I couldn't help but grin at their infectious enthusiasm.

Sundowners and Sunset Splendor

Our first drive commenced as the sun descended, casting an orange-pink glow across the sky. A magical light that seemed to ignite the acacia trees and elongate the shadows of the tall grasses bathed the landscape. Martin skillfully parked our open-air Land Rover on a flat clearing, declaring with a flourish, "Time for sundowners!"

It was as if, by ritual, we had hopped out and made ourselves comfortable. Martin had arranged a small table laden with various drinks: local beer, sparkling soft drinks, and the ever-inviting Amarula liqueur—a creamy, exotic treat distilled from the marula fruit. I raised my glass, savoring the cool sip, taking in the spectacle before me. The sunset transformed the sky into a masterpiece of purples, golds, and deep oranges, each color bleeding into the next. It was like the entire horizon was a canvas for an artist who had discovered every shade of wonder.

Even in that tranquil moment, my thoughts darted to Jeff. I briefly wondered what he might be doing back in Johannesburg, though the

71

overwhelming majesty of the setting quickly eclipsed the thought. "Don't let distractions steal the moment," I told myself, even as I admired the landscape's interplay of light and shadow.

Night Drive Adventures

With dusk giving way to a star-studded night, we piled back into the Land Rover for a night drive that promised secrets only the dark could unveil. Our ranger, Simon, a quiet and seasoned expert, manned a powerful spotlight that cut through the blackness like a beam from another world. The air was crisp, carrying a subtle chill that made us draw our jackets tighter as we continued along sandy, winding tracks. The symphony of crickets and the occasional call of an owl set the stage for what was to come.

Without warning, Simon hushed us with a sharp gesture, angling his spotlight toward the tall, whispering grass. In the shimmering beam was a leopard—its rosette-patterned coat catching the light and creating an almost surreal, moving mosaic. A collective gasp rippled through our group as we watched the magnificent feline pause, ears twitching as it assessed the situation. Time seemed to hold its breath for a few heartbeats before the leopard silently melted into the darkness, leaving us all in awe.

Our night drive continued to unveil the park's hidden life. A hyena, its nose pressed to the ground in a determined sniff, ambled across the path, while high above, a bushbaby flitted from branch to branch with a comical, almost mischievous agility. At one point, as we rounded a gentle curve, the beam of Simon's spotlight illuminated a pride of lions resting in a clearing. Like tiny, reflective lamps, their eyes twinkled in the darkness, and these apex predators' calm, powerful presence filled us with exhilaration and respect. "It's moments like these that remind you—nature is in charge here," Simon murmured, his voice low and reverent.

The night drive was nothing short of magical, a covert glimpse into a secret world that only came alive when most people were fast asleep in their beds. Every rustle, every whisper of the wind, hinted at a story waiting to be told in the language of the wild.

Dawn of a New Day

Day two greeted us with the soft light of dawn, the horizon slowly unfolding in hues of peach and pink. In our camp, the gentle call of early birds mingled with the soft rustling of the wind as we all reluctantly peeled ourselves from sleep. Over quick cups of strong coffee brewed in the camp's humble kitchenette, we gathered our gear and piled back into the Land Rover for another early morning game drive—when the bush is most enchanting.

The morning drive was a veritable parade of nature's finest. There were birds of every size and description. I had never thought much about birds, but now I realized how varied and unique they are and became aware of their notable personalities.

We soon encountered a majestic herd of elephants at a watering hole, their enormous forms silhouetted against the soft morning light. I watched in rapt attention as one baby elephant, barely taller than a knee, clumsily mimicked the adults—splashing its tiny trunk into the water with an endearing determination. "Isn't that the cutest thing?" whispered someone from behind, and we all shared in the moment of pure, unbridled joy.

Further along, elegant giraffes strolled by, their long necks gracefully reaching to nibble on the tender leaves of towering acacia trees. The sight was almost poetic, each movement deliberate and slow, as if they were the very embodiment of the ancient rhythm of the bush. Meanwhile, hippos lazed on the riverbanks, half-submerged in the cool water, blissfully indifferent to our presence. On the open plains, we witnessed flurries of activity—a medley of springbok, zebra, gemsbok, waterbuck, wildebeest, hartebeest, tsessebe, and even the elusive sable antelope, all coexisting in a vibrant dance of life.

On the Corner of Coetze and Klein

Every click of the camera shutter felt like capturing a slice of an epic saga. Ren and Carla, the determined photographers, were busy angling for that perfect shot. At the same time, Lucy, perched on the edge of her seat, confided to Mark in a hushed tone, "This is more romantic than any honeymoon I could've imagined." In the back, Saeed joked about sending postcards that boasted his safari adventures, and Akiko and I exchanged wide-eyed glances, silently vowing to soak up every extraordinary moment.

Then, as if straight out of a dream, our Land Rover slowed to a halt near a sunlit patch of the savanna. A pride of lions—majestic, serene, and utterly awe-inspiring—had wandered right up to us. They settled so close that their slow, rhythmic breathing vibrations seemed almost audible. One of the larger males, with a mane that glowed in the soft light, sprawled beside the vehicle, his massive head resting against the running board. I was transfixed; each twitch of his ears, each flick of his tail, was a masterclass in nature's quiet power.

In that surreal moment, time stretched on endlessly. My heart pounded, and I felt that even the tiniest sound from our Land Rover might disturb the fragile peace. The driver did not move the Land Rover until the lion decided to get up from his nap. We all sat silently, united in an unspoken understanding that we were mere guests in this wild domain—a domain where nature's rules were absolute and every moment was a lesson in humility and wonder. "I feel so small yet so connected," I thought, marveling at how even the slightest movement of these magnificent creatures could command such profound respect.

Bush Dinners and Campfire Stories

As dusk descended again, our tour organizers surprised us with a bush dinner under a sky bursting with stars. We ambled to a clearing transformed into an outdoor dining haven, where rustic charm met modern comfort. String lights crisscrossed overhead, and candles flickered on linen-draped tables, creating an intimate and celebratory ambiance. Chefs worked at open fires, and their skill was evident in the sizzling sound of grilling meats and roasting vegetables. The smoky aroma was intoxicating, making our stomachs rumble with anticipation.

We dined on various delicious local dishes—succulent game meats, freshly baked bread, and spicy chakalaka relish that danced on the palate. For dessert, a generous serving of sweet, sticky malva pudding arrived, its warm, comforting flavors perfectly complemented by a robust selection of South African wines. Between bites and clinks of our glasses, the gentle murmur of conversation blended with the ambient sounds of the African night: distant howls, a soft breeze rustling through the canopy of trees, and the melodic chirp of crickets.

Lucy excitedly pointed out the Southern Cross constellation as Mark fumbled with his phone's stargazing app, trying to identify every star. I found myself leaning back in my chair, mesmerized by the clarity and intensity of the starlight—a brilliance that no city sky could ever offer. "It feels like we're the only souls in the universe tonight," I remarked, half-joking, half in awe, and the others nodded in silent agreement.

After dinner, we returned to camp, reluctant to leave the magic of the evening behind. A small campfire burned near our rondavels, and as we gathered around its warm glow, stories began to flow as freely as the drinks. Tales of past safaris, humorous mishaps with local wildlife, and even a few ghost stories from the bush punctuated the night. Despite our varied backgrounds and different tongues, laughter and shared amazement knitted us together into an impromptu family under the African sky.

Into the Deep of the Night

Later that night, as the camp quieted and the stars took full command of the sky, I retreated to my rondavel. The room was simple but surprisingly comfortable. I sat on a low wooden bed, the gentle creak of its frame harmonizing with the

77

soft nighttime sounds outside. Through the open window, I could hear the distant call of a nightjar and the rustle of the bush—a lullaby uniquely African. The interior of the rondavel, lit by a single lantern, evoked a sense of adventure and profound comfort. I marveled at how a structure built with such simplicity could shield me from the vastness of the wild while still connecting me to its pulse.

As I lay down, I replayed the day's events—the playful banter in the bus, the surreal encounters on the game drive, the quiet majesty of the lions, and the soulful conversation around the campfire. There was an undeniable thrill in sleeping in the bush, where the line between dream and reality blurred beneath the whispering acacia trees. Every creak and distant rustle promised more wonders to come and was a gentle reminder of nature's ever-present mysteries.

Lingering Thoughts of Jeff

Amid all this awe, my thoughts occasionally strayed to Jeff. I'd tried several times to dismiss the feeling—after all, here in the heart of Kruger, the lions, birds, elephants, and star-studded skies held my full attention. But sometimes, when a particularly stirring scene unfolded—a lion's yawning stretch or the delicate splash of a baby elephant's trunk—I'd glance at my phone, hoping for a message from him. Alas, the cell service in the bush was as elusive as a ghost, and the silence of my screen only deepened my daydreams of him. I wondered if he missed me too or if perhaps he was immersed in a completely different world. Each thought of Jeff was like a gentle tug at my heart, reminding me that the human connections I cherished remained ever-present even amidst the wild.

Farewell to Kruger

We gathered our belongings on the third day, with heavy and full hearts, and piled back into the bus. The drive back to Johannesburg was quieter than our earlier journeys—a reflective silence had taken root in us as we replayed the wild magic we'd witnessed over the past days. I rested my head against the window, the constant vibration of the bus, a soothing metronome that accompanied my reflections. I remembered the low growl of a lion echoing through the darkness, the soft splash of water as an elephant bathed, and the surreal sight of candlelit dinners under the vast African sky.

The photos on my camera were vivid proofs of our adventures—close-ups of elephants with wise, gentle eyes, snapshots of zebras in perfect symmetry, and group photos of us grinning, our faces smeared with dust and wonder. Each image was a tangible piece of a journey that had forever altered the way I viewed the world—and myself. The realization hit me: I had experienced a saga written by nature far richer than any scripted movie or carefully edited travel blog could ever convey.

Returning to Johannesburg felt like stepping back into another world entirely. The city greeted us with blazing sunshine and the familiar hum of urban life—a stark contrast to the quiet majesty of Kruger.

A Familiar Face, A Welcome Sight

I eagerly anticipated disembarking at the Landrost Hotel and sinking into a soft bed; my body tired, but my soul still alight with memories of the wild. However, something unexpected caught my eye as the bus approached the curb.

I squinted in disbelief as my heart skipped a beat—it was Jeff. There he stood, hands tucked nonchalantly into his pockets, exuding that same confident, relaxed charm that had captivated me from the moment we first met. When his eyes met mine, his face broke into a playful grin, and in that instant, all the wild adventures of the past days meshed with a tender, human connection.

"Hi," I managed, my voice betraying excitement and nervous energy. "What are you doing here?"

Jeff's grin widened. "Once again, making sure you eat." he replied with a playful lilt, his eyes twinkling with gentle mischief. He took my travel bag from me as though it were an unspoken promise of further adventures. "I know just the place. And tonight, you can tell me every thrilling detail about Kruger."

I laughed, feeling a warmth spread across my cheeks as I realized how natural it was to slip back into our easy banter. It was as though the rugged wilderness and its epic encounters had woven themselves into my very being. Yet, here he was—a bridge between the wild unknown and the comforting familiarity of home. "After three days of gourmet bush cooking and starlit nights, I'd kill for a hamburger," I teased, half in jest, half in earnest.

Jeff's eyes softened as he replied, "Well, let's make sure no murders happen on my watch." His light yet sincere humor melted away any lingering weariness from the safari. The group from the bus exchanged final goodbyes, each traveler preparing to scatter to their corners of the globe—from London to Sydney, Dubai to Tokyo. But in that final moment, as I stood beside Jeff amid the bustling streets of Johannesburg, I realized that the memories we'd forged together in the wild would forever tie us in a way that transcended language, culture, or geography.

The city hummed around us, yet my mind kept replaying the sights and sounds of Kruger—the gentle snort of an elephant, the soft padding of a lion, the communal laughter around a campfire under the endless African night. I felt a mixture of exhaustion and exhilaration, a bittersweet farewell to a place where nature humbled and inspired me.

And as Jeff linked his arm with mine, inviting me to share his next meal and perhaps the next chapter of my journey, I understood that while the wild magic of Kruger might recede into memory, its lessons would stay with me forever.

"Come on," Jeff said softly, a secret smile playing on his lips as he began walking into the hotel, "I've been waiting a while to see you."

With the warm glow of Johannesburg juxtaposed against the vivid, lingering images of the bush, I felt ready for whatever came next. Whether it was the roar of a lion echoing in the twilight or the murmur of a heartfelt conversation with someone who understood me, life balanced the wild with the wonderfully familiar. And so, with a light heart enamored of exotic animals and starlit nights, I stepped forward into a new adventure.

Chapter 6
Deeper Connections

"I figured you might need some clean clothes." Jeff's tone was light and teasing as he gestured toward my khakis—now stained a deep, earthy red from the dusty trails of the park. I glanced down at them, amused at how they seemed to have absorbed every bit of our adventure. He reached for my small backpack in one swift, almost choreographed motion. I managed a feeble protest—half in embarrassment, half in habit—but his gentle insistence quickly silenced my words.

"Hotel laundry services cost a fortune," he remarked with that mischievous twinkle in his eyes that I'd come to adore. "Let me handle it. My maid will have it done by tomorrow."

I paused a swirl of thoughts inside me. A small, stubborn voice always whispered about my independence, insisting that I should manage my messes. Yet, as I looked into Jeff's sincere gaze, I couldn't help but feel the warmth of his genuine care. It wasn't a flashy gesture or an act meant to impress—it was him looking out for me in the way he naturally did.

"You sure?" I asked, my tone laced with playful reluctance, more out of habit than genuine hesitation.

With an easy shrug, he waved off my concern. "Of course. Consider it a welcome-back gift. After a long, dusty safari, you deserve a little pampering. Now, get cleaned up for dinner. I'll wait for you at the bar." His smile was infectious, and I laughed with him before I knew it.

After a quick shower that washed away the lingering traces of the wild, I changed into a fresh set of clothes. The fabric of my now-clean khakis felt like a gentle reminder of comfort and a stark contrast to the rugged adventures of the day. I met Jeff in the lobby bar, and as we stepped out together, our conversation began to weave its subtle magic.

"Where to tonight?" I asked as we strolled toward the quieter part of town. The evening air was mild, inviting leisurely steps and thoughtful pauses. Streetlights flickered on one by one, casting soft pools of light on the pavement while a gentle breeze played with the hem of my jacket.

Jeff grinned, his eyes dancing with the promise of an undiscovered gem. "I know a little side street where the real heartbeat of the city is felt—not the bustling tourist traps, but the small, unassuming eateries that locals swear by."

On the Corner of Coetze and Klein

I couldn't help but agree. "I love those places. They have character and a story all their own."

The world around us felt intimate as we wandered along the side street. We passed by quaint storefronts and small cafés where the aromas of freshly baked bread and rich coffee mingled with the cool night air. Eventually, we slipped into a casual café boasting a simple menu of local dishes with a few international twists. Our table was near an open window, and I could feel the night air brushing softly against my cheek as we settled in.

The background was a pleasant symphony of street sounds—the low hum of conversations in Afrikaans, the distant rumble of a taxi, and even the gentle laughter of friends greeting each other on the sidewalk. The ambiance was relaxed, letting us let our guards down and share more than usual with a casual acquaintance.

"So, tell me about Vegas," Jeff said after a few minutes of sipping his coffee. His tone was curious and warm, inviting me to open up about a world that felt far removed from this quiet corner of the world.

I leaned back in my chair, smiling as I recalled the neon-drenched nights and the relentless pace of life in Las Vegas. "Well, I run a model agency there, and managing it sometimes feels like being a ringmaster in a circus," I began, my voice taking on a conversational lilt. "Imagine organizing massive conventions where thousands of people gather, all buzzing with energy, and then realizing that there's a whirlwind of logistics and planning behind the glitter and glamour. It's exhilarating, exhausting, and occasionally downright chaotic."

Jeff listened intently, resting his chin on one hand as if he were memorizing every detail. Now and then, he interjected with thoughtful questions. "Do you ever find that constant buzz draining?" he asked softly, his eyes probing with genuine concern. "How do you keep it all together when the chaos peaks?"

I chuckled, admitting, "Honestly, sometimes it does feel like juggling flaming torches while riding a unicycle. But there's a thrill in it too—a sense that I'm right where I'm supposed to be, even if it's a bit maddening sometimes."

The conversation flowed naturally, our voices mingling with the ambient chatter of the café. It wasn't long before Jeff began sharing snippets of his own life. "I have two sons," he said, his voice softening as he spoke. "My oldest is almost twelve, and my little guy is eight. They're my world, you know?" His eyes lit up tenderly as he continued, "My older one is absolutely mad about cricket. I never cared much for the sport until I saw him on the pitch. It's as if the rest of the world fades away when he's playing. Fatherhood changes you in ways you never expect."

I found myself drawn to the subtleties in his expression—the way his gaze softened, how his hand absentmindedly ran through his dark hair as he gathered his thoughts. There was a timeless quality to his kindness; simple acts like carrying my bag or opening the door felt imbued with an old-fashioned gallantry that was both refreshing and deeply reassuring. For a woman who had always prided herself on forging her path, this gentle attentiveness felt like a safe harbor in a chaotic world.

As the night deepened, our conversation meandered through a tapestry of subjects. We traded stories about our favorite movies, recounted odd travel anecdotes, and debated the merits of various late-night snacks. It was as if time had slipped away unnoticed—one moment, we were immersed in discussions about the vibrancy of Las Vegas, and the next, we were laughing about silly mishaps from our respective pasts.

When we finished dinner, I glanced at my watch in disbelief. "Have we been talking for hours?" I marveled. Jeff only smiled, his eyes crinkling at the corners as he replied, "Time flies when you're with someone who makes every minute count."

As we left the cozy confines of the café, the streets outside were quieter now, the occasional car passing by in the soft glow of streetlights. The night air retained a lingering warmth, reminiscent of a summer that refuses to say goodbye too soon. We strolled back to the hotel, our conversation ebbing and flowing effortlessly—from deep reflections about life to lighthearted banter about the quirks of our daily routines.

We lingered for a moment, a comfortable silence filled with unspoken possibilities. Eventually, Jeff stepped aside, allowing me to head toward the elevator. As the sliding doors closed behind me, I leaned against the wall, letting my thoughts wander. The day's events swirled in my mind: the thrill of returning from the wilds of Kruger, the unexpected comfort of seeing Jeff waiting for me, and the sweet rush of discovering layers of connection that had only begun to unfold.

In that quiet moment, I reflected on how Jeff had shown me a thoughtful and remarkably gentle side of himself. His stories about his sons, how he described the simple joys of fatherhood, and his readiness to offer a hand—even for something as trivial as carrying a backpack—spoke to a deep, abiding kindness. It was a side of him that felt rare and precious, almost as if it belonged to a bygone era where small gestures meant the world.

I thought, "In a world full of fleeting encounters, maybe some connections are meant to be nurtured, cherished even." It was a comforting thought that made the uncertainties of travel and chance meetings seem worthwhile.

I made a quiet promise to myself—to be open to the unexpected, to cherish the small gestures, and to let the natural flow of life guide me, even when it led me far from the familiar neon lights of Vegas into a world where genuine connections blossomed under the soft glow of evening streetlights.

I took a deep breath in my hotel room as I finally opened the door. An unusual calm settled over me—starkly contrasting the hectic pace of my usual routine after a big trip. Instead of the usual rush to check messages or plan the next move, my thoughts centered on Jeff.

Lying in bed that night, I replayed our conversation over and over in my mind—the easy flow of our words, the laughter we shared, and the gentle way he had guided our talks from casual to deeply personal. I realized that sometimes it wasn't the grand gestures but these quiet, thoughtful moments that genuinely built a bridge between two hearts.

Chapter 7
Weekend Escapes and a Surprise Caller

Saturday morning was unplanned, so I decided to go down to the restaurant for breakfast. Upon entering the lobby, the front desk manager smiled warmly and held out a large paper bag. "Ma'am," he said, "someone dropped this off for you earlier."

Curious, I took the bag and raised an amused eyebrow. Opening it, I discovered my freshly laundered clothes—each piece neatly folded and imbued with the faint scent of detergent and, perhaps, a whisper of lavender. Nestled atop the folded khakis was a small handwritten note, the neat cursive spelling out: "Dinner tonight? —Jeff." My heart did a little flip at the simple invitation. In a world dominated by digital messages and fleeting texts, receiving a handwritten note carried a nostalgic charm that felt profoundly personal.

I glanced up to find Jeff looking at me, his hands casually tucked into his pockets and a hopeful quirk playing at the corners of his mouth as if expecting an answer. Our eyes met, and in that silent exchange, there was an unspoken acknowledgment of the connection we were nurturing—a feeling that perhaps this was something real and worth exploring.

"Thanks," I managed to say softly, holding up the bag as if to emphasize my gratitude. "You didn't have to do all this."

He shrugged as if it were the simplest thing in the world. "I enjoyed it," he replied earnestly. "Besides, it gave me an excuse to see you this morning. If you don't have any plans, how about spending the day with me? Surely you can trust me to drive you by now," he teased. "I brought back your clothes."

I couldn't help but laugh at his gentle banter, the memory of him whisking away my dusty safari gear for laundering still fresh in my mind. Slipping into the passenger seat, I settled in and let the ease of our morning routine take over. As we merged into the light traffic, I observed how the city on the weekend had a different pulse—there was a languid vibe in the air, as if even the streets were taking a well-deserved break. Music drifted from the open doors of corner shops, mingling with the tantalizing aroma of fresh curries, sizzling street foods, and warm pastries.

"So, any plans for today besides my stellar company?" Jeff quipped, glancing at me with a playful smirk as we drove on.

"Hmm," I replied with a smile, "maybe if you promise more of those witty remarks, I might consider sticking around a bit longer."

We soon reached the bustling Indian market as the sun climbed high, casting a golden glow over everything. Stall after stall burst with vibrant color: brilliantly patterned saris fluttered in the breeze, gleaming bangles neatly stacked, and shelves overflowed with fragrant spices and teas. The air was alive with the chatter of vendors and the clink of coins, and every corner promised a new sensory delight.

Jeff and I wandered slowly through the market, stopping frequently to admire the displays and sample the local treats. At one stall, an elderly vendor offered us a taste of sweet, syrupy jalebis while extolling the virtues of her secret spice blend. "You simply must try my masala chai," she insisted in a friendly tone, handing me a tiny cup that warmed my hands as much as my heart.

Between bites of spicy samosas and sips of the aromatic brew, we laughed over our attempts to learn the local lingo. "Namaste, or is it 'Hello, how's it going?'" Jeff attempted a greeting in Hindi, only to mix in a stray Afrikaans word mid-sentence. I laughed, teasing him gently, "That was a delightful cocktail of languages, Jeff! You might start a new trend." I fumbled with my attempts at local slang, and soon, we were both giggling at our humorous mispronunciations.

The conversational rhythm between us felt natural and unforced. Vendors who caught our laughter would join in, complimenting our "exotic" attempts at speaking their language. We collected little treasures along the way—a packet of spicy masala tea here, a set of decorative bangles there. Each purchase felt like a shared secret, a small token of the day's adventure.

When we finally decided to leave the market, our hands were full and our spirits high. "Hungry?" Jeff asked as he tossed our market treasures into the back seat with a flourish. My stomach gave a hearty growl in response. Despite having sampled plenty of market snacks, I yearned for something more substantial—a proper meal that satiated both hunger and our shared appetite for new experiences.

"I have another idea," Jeff said, steering the car onto a quieter suburban road. His voice carried that familiar blend of confidence and warmth. "How about dinner at my place? Nothing fancy, but I'm a decent cook... or so I'm told."

The invitation sent a delightful thrill through me. Something about Jeff's casual assurance, his knack for turning ordinary moments into memorable ones, made me say yes before I even had a chance to consider the logistics. "That sounds perfect," I replied, and his eyes lit up as if he'd been waiting for me to agree.

His home was in a leafy suburb—a charming neighborhood where tall jacaranda trees cast lacy, dappled shadows on the pavement. A low brick wall framed the property, and vibrant red bougainvillea tumbled over the entrance like a welcoming cascade of color. The moment we stepped inside, I felt an immediate sense of ease. The living room exuded a cozy warmth, decorated with beautifully carved furniture and dotted with souvenirs from Jeff's travels. There were wooden masks from West Africa, intricately carved sculptures from Zimbabwe, and potted ferns that danced in the gentle afternoon light streaming through expansive windows.

We entered the kitchen, where the atmosphere shifted into playful collaboration. Jeff handed me a cutting board as we began to prepare dinner together. "You chop, I'll handle the spices," he declared, his tone light and conspiratorial. Soon, we were laughing over shared mistakes—an onion cut too thick here, a tomato that squirted its juice unexpectedly there—while the air filled with the heady aroma of cumin, onions, and simmering tomatoes.

Between stirring fragrant mixtures and carefully tasting the sauce, our conversation deepened. "I love these conversations," I said as I passed a bowl of freshly chopped vegetables. "It's like we're in our little world here."

Jeff smiled, pouring a generous measure of wine into two glasses. "I agree. Sometimes, the best adventures are the ones that happen right in your kitchen," he replied, clinking his glass gently against mine.

The conversation naturally drifted into more intimate territory, and as the evening unfolded, our laughter became quieter and our glances more meaningful. We discussed childhood memories, shared little regrets, and exchanged hopes for the future. There were moments when the conversation dipped into comfortable silences—each pause laden with unspoken understanding. After dinner, as we moved to the living room and settled into the warm embrace of soft cushions, our arms gradually found each other. There was no explosive declaration or dramatic spark, like puzzle pieces quietly fitting together. It felt natural, as if the universe had gently nudged us toward this moment.

The following day, I awoke in his sunlit living room, still nestled among the soft cushions of his well-worn couch. The early light painted everything in a golden hue, and I could see Jeff in the kitchen, busy brewing coffee. We exchanged easy, sleepy smiles that needed no words—a silent acknowledgment of the shared passion from the night before.

Then, unexpectedly, my phone buzzed. I glanced at the screen, and my heart skipped a beat when I saw Vimmi's name. His usually upbeat voice now carried a concern that tugged at my heart.

"Sarah!" his voice rang out as soon as I answered. "Where have you been? Mom and I have been worried about you. We want to take you to Sun City! You have to come. Please say yes!"

I paused, feeling mixed emotions as I listened to Vimmi's excited yet anxious rambling. Sun City—a name that resonated with grandeur and promises of luxurious escapes—was a famous resort known for its casinos, golf courses, and live entertainment. Vimmi went on, apologizing profusely for leaving me to explore Johannesburg alone for so long, then insisting that I join him and Marti for a weekend getaway. They were incredibly excited about catching a Julio Iglesias performance, a name that somehow evoked mystery in my mind.

Jeff, who had been quietly listening from the doorway, raised an eyebrow when he heard the details. "Go," he said, his tone calm and supportive as he touched my shoulder warmly. "Experience more of the country. I'll still be here when you get back."

A pang of reluctance shot through me. I had only begun to discover the deeper layers of connection with Jeff—those tender moments in the kitchen, the shared laughter, the comforting silence after dinner, the intense lovemaking. The idea of stepping away, even temporarily, felt like breaking the gentle rhythm we'd started to build. Yet, there was a spark of curiosity about Sun City—a chance to experience another iconic slice of South Africa alongside Vimmi and Marti.

After a few moments of quiet reflection, I made my decision. "I'll go," I said softly, my voice a mix of excitement and a touch of wistfulness. Jeff nodded, understanding without a word the complexity of my feelings.

With a final ride back to the Landrost Hotel, Jeff drove me with a gentle silence that spoke volumes. When we arrived, he helped me hoist my things into Vimmi's waiting car. Before I stepped away, I turned to him and whispered, "Thank you for everything—the market, the dinner, the laughter. I'll be back before you know it."

He smiled warmly and brushed his hand lightly against my cheek as if imprinting that touch into my memory. "Have a great time," he said, his voice soft yet firm, "and come back soon."

As I drove away with Vimmi and Marti, the cityscape blurred past, my mind flickering between the promise of a new adventure and a gentle ache at leaving Jeff behind—even temporarily. I replayed our conversations, the easy camaraderie, and the quiet intimacy of the night before. There was something undeniably magical about these moments—a reminder that sometimes, during travel and surprise calls, you find parts of yourself you never knew were missing.

On the Corner of Coetze and Klein

The day ahead promised new experiences at Sun City, but deep down, I couldn't help but wonder when I'd next share a quiet morning coffee with Jeff or laugh together over a playful attempt at local slang. And even as the road took me away from him, a part of my heart stayed behind, cherishing every shared smile and whispered secret that had made our weekend escape so unexpectedly unforgettable.

Chapter 8
Sun City, Julio, and Unwashed Cheeks

Vimmi's mother, Marti Patterson, was a striking figure who still carried the poise and confidence she'd perfected as one of South Africa's top models. There was an effortless grace to how she tilted her chin or tossed her head to shift a stubborn strand of flaming red hair away from her eyes. That hair— she used to joke—was every designer's dream and her curse: it made her impossible to miss on the runway and equally impossible to hide on a bad hair day. Even now, years after trading the catwalk for family life, Marti's presence filled every room she entered. Friends swore it was the glow in her wide green eyes or the lingering remnants of that confident, modelesque posture she'd honed over decades. Vimmi thought it was his mother's sheer love of life that radiated outwards, uncontainable energy pulsing with every graceful step she took—as if she'd never left behind the adrenaline of the runway.

When Marti heard that Vimmi was coming home for a visit, she practically erupted with joy. And if he brought someone along, well, the more the merrier was her motto. She had already started mentally planning the welcome dinner, dialing up old friends and promising them an evening full of laughter, fine food, and spirited reminiscences of her glory days in the modeling world. The fact that her son's traveling companion happened to be his client—a bright-eyed model agency director freshly arrived from Vegas—made the occasion even more exciting in her eyes. To Marti, every new face was an opportunity to share her favorite South African dishes and pepper her conversation with hilarious stories of her past, each ending with contagious laughter that left everyone begging for more.

When we arrived in South Africa, Marti had greeted us with arms flung wide, speaking in a rapid tumble of Afrikaans and English. Half-laughing, she tripped over her excitement as she whisked Vimmi and me out of the terminal and into her car. In no time, she had driven us to the Landrost Hotel in downtown Johannesburg, where they had dropped me to fend for myself until this very day.

Vimmi was an impressive sight—standing at six-foot-two with a lean, athletic 190 pounds of sculpted muscle. Years spent rehearsing as a professional dancer in Las Vegas had paid off, as his presence lit up any room he entered. Quick to laugh, his smile was almost magnetic, turning heads wherever he went. It didn't hurt that on top of his striking looks, he exuded natural charisma. His easy manner of speaking and exotic accent drew people in before they knew what hit them. And his talents didn't stop on the dance floor; Vimmi was launching a career in glamour photography, with an uncanny knack for capturing that perfect angle, expression, and interplay of light that made his subjects shine.

Ironically, though, it was hard not to suspect that sometimes the real show was the photographer himself. Born in South Africa and raised in a family of linguists, Vimmi spoke eight languages (plus a few African dialects he'd picked up along the way) and would switch mid-sentence from English to Afrikaans or French, leaving everyone around him enchanted. Between his linguistic gift and his dancer's grace, he wore charm as naturally as one might wear a signature fragrance—a subtle, irresistible aura that lingered long after he had passed by.

The drive from Johannesburg to Sun City began perfectly enough. Marti took the wheel, humming an upbeat tune that filled the car with cheerful energy. I sat in the passenger seat, gazing at the rolling landscape and mulling over the glitz and glamour promised at our destination. Vimmi lounged in the back, dispensing chocolate bars and other assorted snacks like a benevolent pied piper of treats. I imagined Sun City as a playground of Las Vegas–style excitement—casinos, flashy entertainment venues, and even the occasional celebrity performance—all set against the stunning backdrop of the South African sun.

As we cruised along the highway, the scenery transformed from the urban sprawl of Johannesburg to vast, open stretches of sunbaked plains dotted with acacia trees. The road became a ribbon of dusty asphalt, bordered by scrubby bushes and the occasional grazing herd of antelope. Our conversation flowed as easily as the passing scenery. Marti regaled us with stories of her younger days on the runway, each anecdote punctuated by a playful toss of her red hair and a dramatic sigh that made us all smile. Vimmi joked about converting the highway into a catwalk for her, and I couldn't help but join in the laughter. The atmosphere in the car was warm, fun, and conversational—a perfect prelude to what lay ahead.

About halfway through our journey, however, the idyllic drive took an unexpected turn. The car began sputtering ominously, and Marti's confident humming became a worried hum. With a sudden jolt, the engine died completely, leaving us coasting to a standstill on the side of the highway. The midday sun was relentless, its heat pouring through the vehicle's roof and turning the interior into a mini sauna.

"Oh dear," Marti sighed dramatically, pushing her oversized sunglasses up on her head with a flourish. "I forgot to fill the tank." Her voice carried a mix of embarrassment and resigned humor that filled the cramped space inside the car. Her words hung in the stale air, and I could practically feel a bead of sweat rolling down the back of my neck. We were officially stranded: no petrol station in sight and miles of flat, open road stretching in both directions. My phone battery hovered slightly above 20 percent—a fragile lifeline—but it was enough. I knew what to do.

"I know who can bail us out," I announced confidently, reassuring Marti and myself that everything would be fine. I dialed Jeff without a second thought. Within seconds, his familiar voice answered, and his calm tone instantly eased my mounting anxiety as I explained our predicament: on the highway, out of fuel, halfway to Sun City, and on the brink of a meltdown.

"Don't move," Jeff instructed firmly. Despite our immobility, his tone was like a promise that help was coming. Less than an hour later, a cloud of dust signaled the arrival of Jeff's car. I caught sight of his vehicle and felt my spirits lift instantly. He pulled up on the shoulder with an extra canister of fuel—a modern-day knight riding to the rescue. Jeff parked behind us, climbed out with a lopsided grin, and tapped the roof of Marti's car.

"Let me guess," he teased good-naturedly, "this beast of a machine runs better on petrol?" His easy banter was the perfect antidote to our earlier tension.

Marti giggled, both embarrassed and relieved. "Thank you, Jeff. I owe you a dinner for this," she said, her voice light as she fanned herself with a crumpled map from the glove compartment.

Jeff waved off her gratitude. "Anytime. Just glad you're all okay." As he expertly poured the fuel into the tank, I stepped aside with Marti, watching how natural and efficient he was in saving the day. His competence—paired with the warm memory of our last evening together—sent a delightful flush through me.

With the tank refilled, Jeff's steady hands brought the engine back to life. Marti turned to Jeff, eyes shining. "Listen, we're going to see Julio Iglesia in concert. You should come with us. We have an extra ticket." Her invitation was warm and genuine.

Jeff hesitated for a moment, glancing at me with an expression that was fond but conflicted. I sensed he was weighing the idea carefully, but eventually, he shook his head softly. "I'd love to, but I don't want to intrude on your plans."

"It wouldn't be an intrusion," I insisted, a flicker of disappointment tugging at me. Even so, I understood his responsibilities in Johannesburg. After briefly exchanging thanks and friendly goodbyes, Jeff returned to his car and drove off. As his car faded into the distance, I couldn't help but wish he'd changed his mind and joined us for the adventure ahead. Sensing my mood, Marti squeezed my hand gently and said, "Don't worry, dear. We'll have a fantastic time."

By the time we reached Sun City, the afternoon sun was beginning its graceful descent, casting the sky in magnificent hues of pink and gold. Sun City was as dazzling as I'd imagined—a resort that combined Las Vegas–style excitement with a distinctly South African flair. The resort sprawled before us like a glittering oasis, its manicured lawns and towering palm trees contrasting sharply with the rugged landscapes we'd left behind. Even though we had encountered a minor roadside mishap, the energy of the place was exciting. People hustled along, laughing and chattering as they went to dinner or the evening's concert venue. Neon signs and vibrant banners hinted at the promise of late-night entertainment and high-rolling casinos.

Unfortunately, our unexpected delay had come at a cost. We missed almost the entire Julio Iglesia concert—leaving Marti utterly devastated. "You don't understand," she wailed dramatically, her voice cracking with emotion, "Those tickets cost a small fortune. I've been dreaming of seeing him live for ages. And I didn't even get a program—I would love to have a program!"

I knew better than to let her wallow in despair. After all, I'd grown up in Las Vegas, where one learns that you can charm your way backstage if you set your mind to it. Switching into "fix-it" mode, I grabbed Marti's hand and said, "Come on. Let's at least try." With determination in my eyes, I led her to the entertainment office. There, I explained our roadside fiasco and how we'd missed the show, asking politely for a concert program to salvage what remained of our evening. The secretary, barely glancing up from her paperwork, produced a program for each of us in no time.

"Now, where do we go to get them signed?" I asked, feeling a surge of adrenaline as the possibility of a backstage encounter materialized.

"Stage door 4," she replied, almost too cheerily.

In a flash, I marched us straight to stage door 4—a nondescript metal entrance guarded by a burly security man who eyed our dusty jeans and T-shirts with melted chocolate smudges (yes, chocolate bars that had transformed into molten lava in our overheated car). A crowd of women was at the door, squealing and trying to get backstage. With more bravado than sense, I fished out a business card from my professional speaking days, pushed through the crowd, handed my card to the security guard, and said in my most authoritative tone, "Please tell him I'm here."

"Tell who?" the security guard asked, raising an eyebrow.

"Julio," I replied, my voice firm despite the situation. My card featured a glamorous headshot of me holding a microphone, complete with a Las Vegas address, which might have made one think I was an entertainer from Sin City.

The guard hesitated momentarily before disappearing inside with my card in hand. Marti shot me a look that mixed admiration with disbelief. "What if he has us thrown out?" she whispered conspiratorially.

I could only shrug, trying to contain my jitters as we waited. Moments later, the guard returned with a distinguished gentleman in a costly, well-tailored suit who motioned us to follow him down a narrow hallway.

Backstage Surprises

We soon found ourselves in a bustling backstage lounge, alive with activity. Reporters jostled about with notepads, waiters in black tails and white gloves gracefully passed trays of champagne flutes and hors d'oeuvres, and a small group of musicians lingered in a post-performance haze of adrenaline. The suited gentleman announced, "Ladies, make yourselves at home. He'll be with you shortly." My heart pounded as Marti and I exchanged excited glances.

Then, Julio entered the room wearing an elegant robe and a welcoming smile. He spotted us immediately, approached with the warm assurance of a seasoned star, and extended his hand in a classic, continental greeting. "You must be Sarah," he said, his voice as smooth and velvety as his stage presence. "Do you mean you came from Las Vegas to see my show?"

"Yes, and we missed it," I blurted out, "because we ran out of petrol. We only got to hear your very last song." I felt my cheeks warm as I explained that the true super-fan was Marti—a woman who had driven hours to see his performance only to miss almost the entire show due to our little mishap. Julio's eyes flicked to Marti, who was practically vibrating with excitement, and his gentlemanly instincts took over.

Before we knew it, he'd whisked her to a baby grand piano in a corner of the room. Sitting down, he serenaded Marti with a snippet of a classic tune, his low, melodic voice filling the room. The surrounding crowd smiled and snapped photos, and Marti was positively over the moon. The highlight, of course, was when Julio planted two chaste but charming kisses on her cheeks—a moment that left her exclaiming, "I'm never washing my face again!" in a mixture of shock and delight.

The entire scene felt surreal—like we'd stepped out of an overheated, dusty car and into a glamorous daydream. There we were, still sporting our travel-worn, chocolate-laden, unwashed clothes while everyone in the room was dressed for an extravagant after-party. Yet, no one seemed to mind our disheveled appearance—not even Julio.

An Unforgettable Resort Day

After our backstage adventure, Marti and I collapsed into our shared hotel room at Sun City, giggling and rehashing every absurd, wonderful moment. "Can you believe this?" she said, pointing at her cheeks in the mirror. "Julio Iglesia kissed me— twice!" Our laughter filled the room, blending the thrill of celebrity encounters with our impromptu exploits.

The next morning, we woke to a brilliant dawn shimmering over the resort's palm-fringed pools and faux beach areas. Stepping outside, the day greeted us with warmth and promised more adventures. Sun City was a wonderland: sparkling water features, sprawling lawns with vibrant flowerbeds, and luxurious villas that overlooked manicured gardens. I marveled at the sight—this was where the glitz of Las Vegas met the relaxed charm of a tropical paradise.

I wondered how anything could top the previous night's excitement—until we stepped outside and spotted Julio himself lounging by the main pool. He lifted a hand in greeting as soon as he caught sight of us, beckoning us over with a grin.

"Sarah, Marti, join me!"

He was every bit as charming by day as he was by night. Over fruit platters and iced coffee, we listened to him chat about his performances, travel schedule, and love of the local culture. A handful of backup dancers emerged, some of whom I knew and had worked for me at my model agency in Vegas. They rushed over with squeals of surprise, and we fell into an impromptu reunion. Their presence and hugs made Sun City feel like a home away from home, bridging the gap between two continents.

We soon discovered that Sun City was more than a resort; it was a playground of endless possibilities. As we strolled along pathways lined with tropical palms and decorative fountains, the air buzzed with laughter and the occasional distant sound of slot machines from a nearby casino. I couldn't help but be charmed by the vibrant mix of people—from families in vacation mode to groups of friends reveling in the high-energy atmosphere. There were live music performances in open-air bars, and the aroma of gourmet street food mingled with the salty tang of poolside cocktails.

Before long, Vimmi declared that we should try parasailing—a wild idea that made me laugh and terrified me. Strapped into a harness and hoisted into the air, we soared above the sparkling waters, the resort's manicured grounds shrinking beneath us. The wind rushed past our faces as we cheered, feeling both exhilarated and ridiculous at our audacity. Later, as we cooled off in the resort pool, sipping neon-colored cocktails adorned with tiny umbrellas, I couldn't help but reflect on how much our day had transformed—from the frustration of a stalled engine to the sheer joy of unexpected adventures.

Marti wore a starstruck smile everywhere we went, still floating on a cloud from her serenade with Julio. I was genuinely delighted for her; there's something magical about watching someone experience their dream moment, even if it comes wrapped in a cocktail of mishaps and spontaneous backstage passes.

Lingering Thoughts of Jeff

Yet amid all the excitement—meeting celebrities, reuniting with friends from Vegas, parasailing over a shimmering resort—I couldn't shake my thoughts of Jeff. I kept replaying the memory of him arriving on the highway with that extra canister of fuel, the steadfast reliability in his eyes as he reassured me that we'd be back on the road in no time. I remembered the subtle tilt of his smile as he politely declined Marti's invitation, not wanting to intrude on what he saw as my adventure. Each recollection sent a quiet flutter through my stomach, a soft reminder of our connection in Johannesburg.

I wondered what Jeff was up to at that moment— perhaps tending to business deals or enjoying a quiet afternoon with his son at a cricket practice session.

Even amid Sun City's dazzling allure, a part of me ached to return to him. The urge to leave the resort immediately, hop in a car (this time with a full tank), and drive straight back to Johannesburg was strong. Yet, I remembered his words encouraging me to explore and experience all that life had to offer, so I resolved to enjoy every moment of our adventure here.

The day melted into a whirlwind of poolside conversations, impromptu photo sessions with Marti and Vimmi, and plenty of laughs as we navigated the vibrant, sun-drenched corridors of Sun City. When evening finally arrived, the resort transformed once again. The sun dipped below the horizon, casting a spectacular array of oranges, pinks, and purples over manicured lawns and sparkling fountains. I found a quiet corner at one of the resort's many restaurants, where Marti and I sat down for dinner. Between bites of exquisitely spiced local dishes and sips of fine wine, we recounted every surreal detail of the trip—from our roadside fuel fiasco and the missed Julio Iglesias concert to our impromptu backstage pass that had led to Marti's unforgettable serenade.

Yet, amid the kaleidoscope of lights, music, and new experiences, my thoughts drifted back to Jeff— the man who rescued us on the highway and left an indelible mark on my heart. Even as I laughed and chatted with newfound friends, I couldn't help but wonder when I'd next see his reassuring smile or feel the warmth of his gentle touch. The day belonged to Julio, Marti, and the thrill of Sun City, but my heart lingered on Jeff. I couldn't wait to return to Johannesburg, see him again, and explore new possibilities between us.

As the night deepened, I sat back and savored the final moments of our unforgettable resort experience. The blend of Vegas showbiz flair and the vibrant soul of Africa had woven together an experience that was as wild as it was tender—a tapestry of misadventures, serendipitous encounters, and unwashed cheeks that would forever remain a cherished memory.

Chapter 9
Family Ties and Future Whispers

We returned to Johannesburg on a bright, clear afternoon, the sunlight dancing across the car's windshield as Marti expertly navigated the final stretch of highway back into the city. There was something immensely comforting about coming back to familiar sights and sounds after the sensory overload of Sun City. And yet, as much as I appreciated the familiarity, a deeper part of me already missed the heady excitement we'd experienced the days before.

The moment our car pulled up to the Landrost Hotel, my heart skipped a beat. There, near the entrance, stood Jeff—hands tucked casually into his pockets, wearing that relaxed, knowing smile that always made my heart flutter a little faster. Without waiting for any formal acknowledgment, he strode over and began helping me unload my suitcase from the trunk. As he leaned in to kiss my cheek softly, he said, "Welcome back," in a warm and reassuring tone. "Let me help you get checked back into the hotel. I have a couple of errands to run, so I'll take care of that while you rest and get dressed for dinner. Then I'll return to take you to that wonderful curry restaurant I told you about. How does that work for you?"

His words were gentle and practical, promising more time together. I smiled in response, feeling the comfort of routine and the thrill of anticipation ripple through me. After a long and leisurely bath that washed away the dust and memories of Sun City, I treated myself to a short, blissful nap. When I finally dressed, I chose a pretty sundress paired with high-heeled, strappy sandals—an ensemble that felt perfect for the evening ahead. I draped a light shawl around my shoulders, letting my hair fall naturally, loose, and carefree as if echoing the freedom I had felt over the weekend.

Later that evening, Jeff arrived—still in his crisp work suit, a testament to his dedication even after a long day. His eyes crinkled in delight as he saw me, and we shared a few light-hearted exchanges. Over plates filled with fragrant curries and freshly baked naan at dinner, I animatedly recounted my adventures at Sun City. I told him about Marti's near-fainting moment when Julio Iglesia planted those unexpected, chaste kisses on her cheeks, how we had soared through the skies parasailing above glittering pools, and how a few of the Vegas dancers—whom I had worked with back in Las

Vegas—had been performing there, adding an extra layer of surreal connection to our time in South Africa. Jeff listened intently, a smile playing on his lips as he chuckled at my animated descriptions. Yet, amidst the laughter and casual banter, I sensed a thoughtful pause behind his eyes—a silent prelude to something more meaningful.

After a lull in our conversation, he leaned forward and said, "I was wondering... Would you like to meet my father and sister? They live in a small town about fifty kilometers from here. We could drive out tomorrow if you'd like."

His invitation took my breath away. In the brief yet intense time I'd known Jeff, I had already seen different facets of his life—how he cared for his family, his unassuming resourcefulness during that memorable fuel fiasco on the highway, and his genuine kindness that shone in every word and action. Now, here he was, offering to open the door to his family and let me step further into his world. I found myself nodding eagerly, my heart racing with excitement and a hint of nervous anticipation.

The following day dawned clear and promising. Jeff picked me up in his trusty BMW, and soon, we were on the open road, leaving behind the urban hum of Johannesburg. The drive was like a journey into another realm—fields of tall, whispering grass and vast patches of farmland whizzed by in a blur of greens and golds. The city's constant buzz gave way to a serene landscape where traffic thinned out, and the road seemed to stretch endlessly ahead. We passed small clusters of pastel-painted shops or roadside stands offering fresh fruit and handmade crafts. Jeff would slow the car long enough for me to pull over and snap a quick picture—a spontaneous pause I knew I would treasure.

As the rolling hills gave way to a quaint, cozy town, I felt a gentle excitement build within me. The town was picturesque, with neatly kept houses accented by vibrant bougainvillea climbing over wrought-iron gates. It was a place where everyone knew everyone else, where life moved at a pace that allowed you to savor every moment. When we finally arrived, Jeff's father was waiting on the front porch of a modest white house. A silver-haired gentleman with kind, wise eyes and an easy, welcoming smile, he exuded an old-world charm that immediately put me at ease. "Welcome!" he said warmly, extending his hand. "I've heard so much about you."

Before I could reply, Jeff's sister burst out of the house, her face radiant with genuine delight. "Sarah! It's wonderful to meet you," she exclaimed, pulling me into an impromptu, heartfelt hug that left me momentarily breathless. In that embrace, I recognized a spark of familial resemblance—a similar twinkle in her eyes to the one I'd seen in Jeff whenever he was pleased.

Inside, the house was a warm, bustling haven. The aroma of a hearty, simmering curry mingled with the inviting scent of freshly baked bread seemed to radiate from every corner. A sturdy dining table laden with bowls of spiced vegetables, succulent roasted chicken, and sweet fruit pies groaned under the weight of a meal prepared with love. We all sat down together, and the conversation flowed like I had always belonged to this close-knit circle. Jeff's father peppered me with questions about life in the United States, the stark contrasts between the deserts of Nevada and the vibrant energy of South Africa, and what had drawn me to this part of the world in the first place. Meanwhile, his sister was curious about my work in the modeling industry, how I found Johannesburg compared to the glitz of Las Vegas, and what kind of adventures had colored my recent journey.

Throughout the meal, little moments spoke volumes. I watched Jeff tease his nieces and nephew with playful jibes, his laughter mingling with theirs in a symphony of familial joy. He gently helped his father locate his misplaced reading glasses, and every so often, his eyes would meet mine, sharing a quick, reassuring smile that made my heart swell with gratitude. This family had an undeniable closeness—a sense of belonging and support that was comforting and inspiring. It was as if every shared story and warm glance were weaving me further into the tapestry of their lives.

After lunch, the family invited us to explore the lush backyard. The sun shone softly over a small vegetable garden that thrived under the African heat. I was charmed when Jeff's young niece proudly showed me a cluster of bright, plump tomatoes she'd been nurturing for a school project. "Uncle Jeff says they taste better than anything from the store," she boasted with a beaming smile, and I couldn't help but admire the innocence and passion in her words.

As we used the family pool and later strolled through the yard that afternoon, I felt a deep connection to Jeff and his entire family. I realized that in witnessing these quiet, everyday moments, I saw a side of him that was far more intricate and endearing than the daring rescuer on a deserted highway. Here, he was a son, a brother, an uncle—a man whose roots were firmly planted in love, tradition, and shared memories. This revelation made me even more curious and hopeful about our future.

As evening approached, we reluctantly prepared to leave the little town behind and return to Johannesburg. The drive was peaceful; the setting sun painting the sky in soft pastels mirrored our car's gentle mood. Just as we were nearing the city, my phone buzzed unexpectedly. Vimmi was on the line, and his voice bubbled with excitement as he asked if I would like to go to Cape Town for a week. Marti had an apartment right on the water near the wharf, and she was inviting Jeff and me to join them there.

I couldn't hide my excitement as I relayed the invitation to Jeff during our quiet ride. He listened thoughtfully, his brow creasing before he declined, explaining that he had important business meetings that week. "But you go," he said with a gentle smile, "Cape Town is the most beautiful city in the world, and you don't want to miss it." His encouragement was warm and supportive. However, I felt disappointed that he couldn't join me on this new adventure.

Vimmi confirmed the plans, saying, "We will pick you up at the hotel in the morning at about nine." That simple arrangement set off a cascade of emotions. Later that evening, Jeff and I shared a light dinner in the hotel's dining room, our conversation punctuated by the soft clinking of cutlery and the low murmur of other guests. After dinner, Jeff stayed overnight with me at the hotel, his presence a comforting anchor amidst the swirling excitement of new plans. When Vimmi and Marti arrived the next morning to take me to the airport for Cape Town, Jeff escorted me down to the car with a tender goodbye. I had already packed a small bag for my Cape Town trip, and Jeff helped me load the bulk of my luggage into his car. "I'll pick you up at the airport when you get back to Johannesburg," he said, his voice soft and sincere, "and if you'd like, you can stay at my place until you depart for the United States."

That promise lingered with me as I drove away with Vimmi and Marti, the horizon ahead shimmering with possibilities. As the familiar hum of the road receded behind me, my thoughts drifted back to the family I had met and Jeff's gentle, unwavering support. There was something profoundly moving about how family ties intertwined with future whispers—a reminder that every goodbye held the promise of a new hello, every moment of connection paving the way for more profound encounters in the chapters yet to come.

Chapter 10
Cape Town Wonders

Arriving in Cape Town felt like stepping into a living, breathing painting. The moment I stepped off the plane, the cool, crisp air wrapped around me—a perfect blend of mountain freshness and a hint of ocean aroma that carried an almost electric energy. Above, the sky unfurled in a brilliant shade of blue so vivid it could have been a postcard. Marti and Vimmi had promised that Cape Town would charm me in ways that even Johannesburg's dynamic pace never could. I knew they were right from the first sight of Table Mountain's majestic silhouette carved against the horizon.

The First Impressions

Cape Town, often celebrated as the floral capital of the world, welcomed me with open arms. The city itself was a tapestry of color and culture. Walking through the streets, I found that every corner told a story—a narrative woven through vibrant murals, bustling markets, and the gentle hum of local chatter. Even the air seemed infused with an artistic spirit as if the city was constantly whispering secrets of its storied past and its promise of adventure.

My temporary home for the next few days was Marti's charming apartment. Nestled on a quaint street across from the promenade, the building was modest and unassuming on the outside, but its interior revealed a world of warmth and style. Bougainvillea cascaded in bursts of magenta and purple over weathered garden walls, and small, colorful flower beds that lent a distinctly Mediterranean vibe to the area ran alongside the walkways. From the balcony of Marti's apartment, I could see a cozy little Greek restaurant on the corner, where locals and visitors gathered for a taste of home-cooked Mediterranean delights. The tantalizing aroma of roasted lamb mingled with hints of garlic and olive oil, creating a sensory invitation I found impossible to resist.

"Come on in; you're going to love it here," Marti said with a smile as she jingled the keys and opened the apartment door. "And wait until you try the moussaka—it's the best in town. Just a hop, skip, and a jump away whenever you get cravings."

Inside, the apartment was awash with natural light. Large windows captured the slanting rays of the morning sun, bathing the living space in a soft, golden glow. Vimmi, ever the enthusiastic traveler, zoomed in behind us. With a dramatic flourish, he dropped his bags in the living room and proclaimed, "Now, this is what I call a holiday!" He flopped onto a plush armchair, his voice bubbling with excitement as if he'd uncovered the secret to happiness.

A Day in the City

From the start, Cape Town exuded a cosmopolitan flair that was impossible to ignore. Marti and Vimmi whisked me away on a whirlwind city center tour the following morning. We strolled through historic streets lined with pastel-colored houses, their facades whispering stories of colonial elegance mixed with modern vibrancy. Upscale boutiques and designer stores dotted the thoroughfares; each window displays a carefully curated work of art featuring the latest Paris fashions. I paused often, mesmerized by elegant dresses that flowed like water, chic handbags that seemed to hold a universe of style, and impeccably tailored suits that spoke of understated luxury.

"You can't leave Cape Town without at least trying one of these on," Vimmi teased, pointing at a sleek black cocktail dress displayed prominently in a boutique window.

I laughed and replied, "Don't tempt me—my suitcase can barely handle what I already have!" Yet, the glint in Marti's eyes and the conspiratorial

127

smiles exchanged between her and Vimmi hinted at the adventures yet to come. Before I knew it, I was trying on garments that made me feel as if I had stepped into a modern fairytale—flowing silks that whispered against my skin, edgy blazers that transformed me into someone daring and new, and a pair of high heels that promised to elevate not only my stature but my spirit. Even if I couldn't bring every piece home, dressing up in these luxurious fabrics filled me with joy.

A Waterfront Lunch

After our impromptu fashion parade, we headed to the bustling waterfront for lunch. The wharf was alive with activity—a delightful blend of locals and tourists all drawn together by the promise of fresh seafood and panoramic views of the harbor. The salty tang of the sea mingled with the irresistible aromas wafting from food stalls and open-air restaurants: grilled fish with a hint of lemon, buttered rolls fresh out of the oven, and sweet pastries that beckoned with each sugary note. Nearby, street performers filled the air with lively tunes, turning the promenade into an impromptu festival of sound and color.

We settled at an outdoor table under a striped canopy at one of the popular waterfront restaurants. As we dived into our meals—crisp calamari drizzled with lemon and a vibrant salad accented with tangy citrus—seagulls swooped overhead, their graceful arcs in the sky punctuating the rhythm of our laughter and conversation.

As I looked around, I marveled at how different Cape Town was from Johannesburg. While Johannesburg thrummed with the pulse of urban energy and a relentless drive, Cape Town exuded a laid-back, coastal ease. Here, the ocean's presence was tangible, weaving a thread of relaxation through every moment. The ambiance was a blend of high-energy sophistication and the unhurried rhythm of the sea ... a duality that felt refreshing and intoxicating.

A Day at the Beach

No visit to Cape Town would be complete without spending a sun-drenched day at its world-renowned beaches. When the weather proved too inviting to ignore, Vimmi insisted we hit the sand immediately. One glance at the dazzling coastline, where pristine white sand met the inviting turquoise waters of the Atlantic, won me over. We unpacked our beach bags and found a quiet spot on the soft sand near the water's edge, where the only sounds were the rhythmic crashing of waves and our lighthearted banter.

Lying on our plush towels, we soaked up the sun's warm embrace and indulged in sweet, fruity granadilla popsicles that cooled us down with every lick. The beach was a lively tapestry of color and movement, with groups of sunbathers, families building sandcastles, and surfers catching the perfect wave. I couldn't help but notice the gorgeous men strolling along the shore—their easy smiles, relaxed confidence, and stylish beach attire turning heads and sparking friendly exchanges. Often, one would offer a friendly wave or a smile, and I found myself laughing and waving back, basking in the simple pleasure of being admired in this coastal paradise.

"They're smiling at me," I declared with a playful grin, pushing my sunglasses onto my head and responding kindly.

Vimmi scoffed good-naturedly, adjusting his wide-brimmed beach hat. "Oh, please. I'm the one drawing all the attention. Just look at these stylish board shorts!"

Our teasing banter continued, each remark more lighthearted than the last, as we both reveled in the warm welcomes of the beach. Whether the complimentary glances were for him or me hardly mattered—it was all part of the carefree joy of being in Cape Town. There was a shared sense of delight in the moment, a feeling that the sun, the sea, and the laughter of new friends could wash away any worries.

Evening Revelations and Teasing

Later that evening, after a day filled with sunshine and salty breezes, we trudged back to Marti's apartment, our skin still warm from the day's adventures and our clothes dusted with remnants of beach sand. But as soon as we entered, we found Marti pacing the living room, her arms crossed over her chest and a playful yet mock-serious expression on her face.

"You've had a phone call," she announced with a dramatic sigh, her tone a mix of amusement and feigned exasperation. "I've lived in South Africa my entire life, and never—never—have I met a man like Jeff. You show up in my country, and what happens? You meet him on your very first day in Joburg. It's not fair!"

A blush of warmth crept over my cheeks at the mention of Jeff. "I'm lucky, I guess," I said, shrugging in a manner that barely concealed the flutter of excitement and a hint of longing that stirred within me every time I thought of him.

"Lucky?" Marti scoffed with a wry laugh. "That's an understatement. You've got all the luck in the world. Believe me, a man like Jeff doesn't come along every day." She perched on the edge of the sofa, her eyes glancing out the window at the twilight sky as if the fading light could hold a secret for her.

Vimmi, never one to let the moment pass without a touch of humor, flopped onto the couch beside her. With a dramatic toss of his hair, he quipped, "Marti, darling, your moment will come. In the meantime, let's all be jealous of Sarah, shall we?" His playful banter had us all laughing, the sound mingling with the hum of the city outside. Despite Marti's teasing, I could see the genuine happiness in her eyes for me, and it comforted me to know that she genuinely celebrated every bit of the unexpected joy Jeff had brought into my life.

Savoring the Flavors of Cape Town

Over the next few days, our schedule was a delightful mix of culinary adventures and scenic explorations. Mornings often began with coffee runs to the charming Greek restaurant on the corner of our block. With a warm smile and hearty "Kaliméra!" greeting, the owner insisted that we try his homemade baklava—a flaky, sweet pastry that melted in your mouth with each nutty, honeyed bite. These small moments of indulgence set the tone for days filled with sensory delights.

Afternoons were for further discoveries. Some days, we returned to the beach, where the rhythmic lapping of waves and the scent of salt in the air reminded us to slow down and appreciate nature's beauty. Other afternoons we spent exploring boutique-lined streets, meandering through vibrant markets, or even embarking on spontaneous drives along the dramatic coastline. The wind would whip through our open car windows, carrying the intoxicating blend of sea air and blooming jacarandas. At the same time, the landscape unfolded in a breathtaking panorama of ocean, mountains, and rugged cliffs.

A Journey Along the Coast

Perhaps the most unforgettable moments came during our coastal drives, transforming a simple road trip into an epic voyage of discovery. We set off from the base of Table Mountain, that iconic flat-topped sentinel that presided over Cape Town like an ancient guardian. As we drove along the Atlantic Seaboard, the scenery shifted dramatically with every mile. Sea Point and Bantry Bay neighborhoods unfurled along the road, a striking contrast of modern luxury against nature's raw beauty. On one side, sleek high-rise apartments and well-manicured gardens hinted at a sophisticated urban life; on the other, the relentless force of the Atlantic waves crashed against rugged cliffs, their power both humbling and awe-inspiring.

Our drive continued through a string of celebrated beaches. Clifton's four crescent-shaped coves, each separated by smooth, time-worn boulders, offered secluded retreats that seemed to whisper promises of private adventures. Nearby,

Camps Bay boasted a palm-lined promenade where trendy cafes and bars spilled laughter and chatter into the twilight. Across the road, the towering peaks of the Twelve Apostles—an extension of Table Mountain's imposing range—rose sharply, framing the vast ocean in a dramatic tableau of rock meeting water.

No coastal drive in Cape Town would be complete without a ride along the legendary Chapman's Peak Drive. Carved into the mountainside like a masterpiece of engineering, the road offered a series of hairpin turns that hugged the cliff face. On one side, sheer rock faces plunged toward the swirling depths of the Atlantic, while on the other, lookout points provided breathtaking vistas of the jagged coastline below. The sound of the surf pounding against the base of these cliffs sent up a mist that glimmered in the sunlight, lending the entire journey an almost surreal quality. At each lookout, we paused in reverence, our eyes taking in the endless stretches of open water, the dramatic interplay of light and shadow on the mountains, and the profound sense of being suspended between land and sea.

As we drove south, the road curved towards the quaint coastal villages of Kommetjie and Scarborough. Here, the pace of life slowed noticeably. These small communities, with their windswept beaches and a steady rhythm dictated by the tides, were a haven for surfers and nature lovers alike.

The ocean's mood seemed to shift in real-time—
whitecaps danced across the turquoise surface
on blustery days, while on calmer days, the water
glistened like polished silver beneath a radiant sun.

Into the Wilderness of the Cape

Leaving behind the urban sophistication of
Cape Town, we soon found ourselves immersed
in the wild, untamed beauty of the Cape of Good
Hope Nature Reserve. This protected area, a rugged
expanse of low-growing shrubs, protea flowers, and
wind-sculpted landscapes, was a living testament
to nature's resilience. The flora and fauna here were
uniquely adapted to the Mediterranean climate,
creating an ecosystem that was as harsh as it was
beautiful. Along the winding roads of the reserve,
we occasionally spotted ostriches strutting with
regal nonchalance, baboons chattering in the trees,
and small antelope darting through the scrub. At
one particularly memorable rest stop, a mischievous
baboon decided that my car was the perfect mode
of transport, clambering onto the hood as if to join
us on our next adventure. Vimmi laughed, saying,
"They often hop on your car and ride into town—
and then hop onto another car later to go back
home!"

Our journey eventually led us to Cape Point,
a place almost mythical in its grandeur. Here, the
rugged cliffs tumbled dramatically down to secluded

beaches fringed by swaying strands of kelp. At the very tip of this promontory, a lone lighthouse stood as a silent guardian against the elements, its beam cutting through the gathering dusk. Some trails wound perilously close to the edge, inviting us to peer down at the frothing, relentless waves crashing against the rocks far below. Standing there, I felt as if I were standing at the very edge of the world, where the might of nature was demonstrable, and all my worldly concerns seemed to vanish into the roar of the ocean.

Although the official geographic boundary between the Indian and Atlantic Oceans is Cape Agulhas, a short distance southeast of Cape Point, many visitors still come to Cape Point to experience the symbolic convergence of these two vast bodies of water. On certain days—especially when the weather shifted unexpectedly—you could see a striking contrast on either side of the point: one stretch of water, dark and tumultuous, evoked the chill of the Atlantic, while the other shimmered with a lighter, warmer hue suggestive of the Indian Ocean's more tropical embrace. It was as if two colossal forces were locked in an eternal dance, their boundaries blurred by the ceaseless energy of the tides.

Standing on the viewing platforms and meandering along the cliffside trails, I felt the power of the wind—a gust that seemed to carry the voices of countless travelers and the echoes of ancient mariners. It was a humbling reminder that I was a small part of a grand tableau where mountains, oceans, and skies converged, displaying nature's unyielding might.

The Return to Urban Life

As dusk approached, we began our journey back toward Cape Town. The transformation of the shoreline was striking. We moved from the sophisticated urban beaches—where modernity met leisure—back to the raw, unfiltered beauty of the southern peninsula. Each turn of the road revealed yet another layer of Cape Town's character, a city that effortlessly blended nature's grandeur with a vibrant cultural scene. When we returned to Marti's apartment, my mind was a whirlwind of impressions: from the hypnotic pull of the ocean's depths to the captivating charm of centuries-old architecture bathed in golden light.

Evenings in Cape Town were a celebration of life. We spent our nights hopping between local restaurants that offered an array of culinary delights—from spicy, aromatic Cape Malay curries to gourmet burgers infused with local flavors. Each meal was an invitation to experience a different facet of the city's rich heritage and cosmopolitan identity. The convivial atmosphere in these establishments, punctuated by friendly chatter and clinking glasses, was a testament to the city's open-hearted spirit.

Reflections on a Magical Place

With each new experience, my amazement at Cape Town deepened. There was something almost magical about how the city blended natural beauty—majestic mountains, endless beaches, and lush gardens—with a dynamic, pulsating cultural scene. Whether I was standing at the edge of the ocean or gazing up at the formidable Table Mountain, I felt an overwhelming sense of reverence, as if the land itself was urging me to explore further, to uncover the layers of history, art, and life that made this place so extraordinary.

Amid the sensory overload of Cape Town's vibrant streets and rugged wilderness, my thoughts often drifted back to Jeff. Every day, his voice on the phone was a welcome reminder of home and of the unexpected connection we had forged. His messages, filled with gentle suggestions of what to see and do, were like secret notes tucked into the fabric of my journey—quiet affirmations that, no matter how far I roamed, he was always with me. And every time Marti teased me about my "lucky" encounter in Joburg, I couldn't help but feel that delightful mix of excitement and longing all over again.

A Tapestry of Experiences

Reflecting on my time in Cape Town, I realized this journey was about much more than sightseeing. It was a vibrant tapestry woven from moments of quiet introspection on sunlit beaches, bursts of laughter during spontaneous shopping sprees, and awe-inspiring encounters with nature's raw power along cliffside roads. I had experienced a modern and timeless city. In this place, every street corner held a promise of discovery, every meal celebrated local flavors, and every sunset painted the sky with hues that defied description.

The drive along the coast, from the bustling urban heart of Cape Town to the wild edges of the peninsula, felt like a pilgrimage to the very soul of Africa. At every turn, the landscape told a story of resilience and beauty—a story that resonated deeply with my journey. From the manicured promenades lined with bougainvillea to the rugged cliffs of Cape Point, where the ocean roared in defiance, Cape Town has shown me that beauty exists in both the cultivated and the untamed.

The Legacy of Cape Town

Even as I prepared to leave this wondrous city behind, I carried an indelible sense of gratitude. Cape Town was a feast for the senses and a transformative experience that reshaped my understanding of what it meant to truly live. In its sunlit streets and wind-swept landscapes, I found a reflection of my desire for exploration—a yearning to embrace every nuance of life, from the simple pleasures of a well-made moussaka to the overwhelming majesty of nature at its most raw.

Returning to Marti's apartment one final evening, as the city lights twinkled like stars in the early night, I sat on the balcony and took one last panoramic view of the skyline. Table Mountain loomed in the distance, a silent sentinel guarding the city's secrets. The ocean stretched to the horizon, a vast, undulating canvas of possibility. In that quiet moment, surrounded by the subtle hum of Cape Town at night, I knew this was a chapter of my life I would never forget—a chapter marked by unforgettable beauty, unexpected friendships, and the thrill of discovery.

Looking Forward

In the days that followed, as I eventually made my way back to Johannesburg and reconnected with Jeff, the memories of Cape Town continued to warm my heart. The city had taught me that adventure was in every corner of the world and that every journey was an opportunity to uncover a new facet of life. Cape Town had opened my eyes to a world of wonder, whether it was the bustling markets, the serene beaches, or the awe-inspiring drives along coastal cliffs.

And so, even as I settled back into the familiar rhythms of Johannesburg, I carried with me the essence of Cape Town—the bright, bold colors, the intoxicating blend of nature and culture, and the unmistakable feeling of having truly lived in a place where every moment sparkled with possibility. Whenever Jeff's voice greeted me over the phone, I would smile, knowing that somewhere in the blend of my past and present, a place existed that had transformed my outlook on life.

The Endless Allure

Looking back, Cape Town was an experience that reshaped my spirit. It reminded me the world is vast and full of surprises, and the magic of discovery often lies in the interplay between nature and human ingenuity. From the tranquil shores of Camps Bay to the wild winds of Cape Point, every scene had been a masterclass in beauty and resilience.

As I continue to travel and explore new horizons, the memory of Cape Town remains a beacon—a reminder of the day when I stood at the world's edge, where mountains, ocean, and sky converged into a grand tableau of wonder. The city's vibrant soul and blend of modern chic and ancient wildness continue to inspire me, urging me to seek beauty in every moment, embrace the unexpected, and always keep exploring.

In the end, Cape Town was everything I'd hoped for and more: a dazzling mosaic of sun-drenched beaches, chic boutiques brimming with couture fashions fresh from Paris, mouthwatering meals that celebrated both tradition and innovation, and nights brimming with laughter, and heartfelt conversations with Vimmi's friends, and the promise of new beginnings. It was a testament to how far I'd come since landing in South Africa—a living reminder that sometimes, the most transformative journeys are the ones that take you far from home into a world where every experience is a brushstroke in the masterpiece of life.

And though I eventually left Cape Town's enchanting embrace to return to Johannesburg and the comforting presence of Jeff, the memories of that vibrant city continue to color my days. Sometimes, when I glimpse a deep blue sky or feel a gentle breeze reminiscent of the ocean, I remember when Cape Town whispered, "You've only scratched the surface." In that quiet reminder, I find the strength to dream of my next adventure, knowing that the world is as vast, unpredictable, and beautifully wondrous as the day I first stepped into that brilliant Cape Town sun.

In its blend of natural splendor, cultural vibrancy, and timeless charm, Cape Town has left an indelible mark on my heart—a mark that continues to inspire every step of my journey forward.

Chapter 11
The Last Days

My final two days in Johannesburg unfolded in a haze of emotion and vivid detail—a tapestry of moments that blurred together like scenes from a tender, half-remembered dream. Every experience instilled a vibrancy that thrilled and softened my heart as if each heartbeat carried a secret farewell. Time seemed to slip away in delicate grains of sand, impossible to grasp fully even as I desperately tried to clutch every precious second. Jeff, ever perceptive and empathetic, appeared to sense the deep well of nostalgia swelling within me. With a quiet determination and gentle insistence, he took it upon himself to transform every remaining hour in this bustling city into something meaningful, a final gift to commemorate the magic of our shared time.

On the first bright morning of those final days, we set out for a sprawling weekend market pulsed with life and culture. The market was already alive under the watchful eye of the high, beaming sun. Yet, the early coolness still clung to the air—a subtle reminder that the crispness of early spring had not yet completely surrendered to the heat of an approaching summer. The market was a vibrant mosaic of sound and color: vendors enthusiastically calling out their wares, the clamor of friendly banter mingling with the soft rustle of handmade goods. As we meandered along the lively alleys, the aromatic interplay of scents filled my senses. The rich, earthy aroma of freshly ground Ethiopian coffee beans wove through the sweeter fragrances of delicate pastries and the piquant, tantalizing scent of samosas spiced with a mysterious blend of herbs.

"Try this," Jeff urged, a spark of excitement in his eyes as he extended a small, carefully handled cup of coffee. This was no ordinary brew—it had been prepared in the traditional Ethiopian style, a process that imbued it with an almost ritualistic reverence. With the first sip, my palate was overwhelmed by a bold, full-bodied flavor that resonated with a quiet intensity, its richness softened by an elusive hint of cardamom. Each taste felt like an awakening, a small celebration of the moment that left me smiling in quiet delight. Jeff's light and genuine chuckle affirmed his pleasure in watching me savor every drop as if it were a precious memory in the making.

We continued to wander through rows of stalls laden with handmade crafts and artisanal treasures. The market was a treasure trove of creative expression: delicate beaded jewelry that caught the sunlight with every movement, intricately hand-carved wooden bowls arranged in neat, artful displays, and brilliant textiles that draped over tables like colorful tapestries telling their own unique stories. Every booth offered a product, a narrative of local heritage and artistic devotion. At one particular stall, Jeff paused by a collection of small sculptures fashioned from twisted wire and vibrant colors. After a thoughtful moment of admiration, he helped me select a small wire sculpture of an elephant—a piece with every curve and twist crafted with painstaking care. "To remember your time here," he murmured as we departed the stall, our hands brushing in a fleeting yet profound contact that spoke volumes of unspoken affection and the gentle bond forming between us.

As the afternoon light mellowed, we made our way to a serene botanical garden nestled on the city's outskirts—a green sanctuary far removed from the clamor of urban life. Passing through ornate wrought-iron gates, we immediately embraced an overwhelming calm. Towering jacaranda trees arched overhead, their delicate purple blossoms falling like confetti onto the lush, manicured lawns below. I tilted my head back to fully capture the spectacle, allowing the filtered sunlight to dance across my face in a pattern of soft, golden hues. The garden exuded an enchanting mix of natural aromas: the rich, damp scent of earth mingled with subtle hints of blooming flowers and the whisper of old memories lingering in the air.

We strolled along a winding, gravel-lined path that beckoned us to explore its secrets. Every so often, we paused to admire the splendor of exotic blooms or to stand in quiet awe at a pond where koi fish glided gracefully beneath the surface dotted with water lilies. The reflective water offered a perfect mirror to the sky, and the gentle murmur of water meeting stone created a soothing background melody. Sometimes, our conversation flowed freely—reminiscing about the vibrant scenes at the market, discussing the fascinating people I had met during my stay, or pondering how abruptly life might shift once I boarded the plane back home. At other times, a comfortable silence enveloped us, filled with the unspoken understanding that sometimes presence and shared experience are more eloquent than words.

The following day, a new burst of activity ushered in a spirited change of pace. Jeff mentioned that his oldest son had a weekend cricket match scheduled at a nearby local field—a game that carried an aura of family pride and communal enthusiasm. Though I had never before watched cricket in person, let alone fully grasped its intricate rules, I enjoyed the prospect of witnessing the game firsthand and sharing in the excitement from the sidelines. The cricket field was a lush expanse of bright green, bathed in the unyielding light of the midday sun. Players in crisp white uniforms moved with a fluid grace against the vivid backdrop. At the same time, clusters of enthusiastic parents and neighbors had set up folding chairs, umbrellas, and picnic blankets along the boundaries, creating a cozy atmosphere of communal celebration.

During the match, Jeff's younger son settled himself between us, his small hand finding mine and holding on with a sincerity that made my heart flutter unexpectedly. From our chosen spot, we cheered and clapped in unison with the crowd, our voices blending with the murmur of excited onlookers. Occasional exchanges of light-hearted jokes and playful commentary with other families punctuated the rhythmic clapping and occasional gasp of anticipation. Every time Jeff's eldest son, tall for his age and brimming with quiet confidence, swung his bat, a crisp crack resonated across the field—a sound that mingled with our collective exhilaration. When he scored a boundary, the crowd erupted in cheers, and I felt the reassuring squeeze of Jeff's hand on my shoulder. His arm, draped around my waist in a protective and tender gesture, reminded me that these shared moments were delicate threads weaving our lives together. In that fleeting instance, I fully embraced the moment's joy, even as the bittersweet realization of an impending farewell loomed like a distant echo.

After the match, as the field slowly emptied and the sun descended toward the horizon, the young cricketer, cheeks flushed with exertion and eyes alight with triumph, jogged back toward us. "Did

149

you see that one?" he called out with infectious excitement, his voice carrying across the gentle din of departing families. His grin, reminiscent of his father's quiet pride, made it impossible not to share in his delight. "I saw!" I replied, my voice tinged with genuine admiration as I beamed back at him. "You were amazing out there!" His contagious happiness seemed to momentarily erase the shadow of parting, letting us revel in a moment of unadulterated connection. We lingered at the edge of the field, conversing with fellow spectators and players alike, the collective joy weaving a temporary cocoon around us. Even though some other families offered a casual post-match gathering, Jeff politely declined, citing "family dinner plans" as the reason. This statement resonated with an unspoken depth that I both cherished and feared.

On the car ride back to Jeff's house, the vibrant energy of the day gradually gave way to a more reflective, subdued mood. The rhythmic hum of the engine became a counterpoint to the silent tension that lingered between us—a tension charged with unasked questions and the weight of impending departure. Neither of us broached the subject of my upcoming flight back to the States, yet it hovered in the air like an unfinished sentence, a secret neither wished to voice. Every so often, I saw Jeff's face in the side mirror, his expression a delicate mixture of resolve and wistfulness, his brow furrowed in quiet contemplation. He sometimes opened his mouth to share his inner turmoil, only to close it again as if the words were too fragile to set free. I recognized the same hesitant fear in my own eyes, a shared apprehension that if we were to voice our thoughts—what if we admitted our longing, our uncertainty about what came next?—we might shatter the delicate spell of these final hours, turning sweet reminiscence into the harsh clarity of goodbye.

By the time we finally pulled into the driveway of Jeff's modest home, dusk had settled into a sky awash with deep oranges, soft pinks, and the gentle purples of twilight. The horizon bled slowly into night, and the once vibrant day now whispered a quiet farewell. The gentle clink of Jeff's keys as he fumbled with the lock felt strangely significant, each metallic note resonating like a subtle heartbeat in the stillness of the evening. Standing on the familiar front step, I watched as he unlocked the door, and the comforting aroma of home—warm, inviting, and rich with the memories of shared moments—welcomed me. It was a scent that mingled the home-cooked essence of past dinners with the faint, lingering trace of Jeff's morning cologne and the undeniable sense of belonging that I had come to treasure.

Neither of us spoke as we stepped inside, yet in that unspoken moment, I could feel a mutual understanding passing between us—a shared recognition that the coming night and the approaching day held an immeasurable value. In a silent gesture loaded with meaning, Jeff reached for my hand, his eyes softly questioning what might come next. I responded with a gentle nod and an equally tender squeeze, a quiet promise that even though time might force us apart, we would choose to spend every moment left with heartfelt intensity and deep gratitude.

That evening, we found ourselves in the kitchen, the space again alive with the familiar rhythm of shared routines. We prepared dinner together as before—chopping vibrant vegetables with deliberate care, the satisfying crunch of fresh produce punctuating the soft murmur of a jazz playlist that filled the background. Each slice of onion or snip of a green pepper felt laden with meaning, a reminder of all the small moments woven into our story. Over bowls of steaming, aromatic curry, our conversation turned to the small but significant details of our day—the playful banter at the market, the way his son's face had lit up after a particularly skillful cricket play, and the tender moment when the younger boy had reached for my hand with all the unspoken hope of belonging. Every shared memory was like a fragile thread connecting us, even as the knowledge of my imminent departure tugged at the edges of my heart.

After dinner, we set out for a stroll through Jeff's neighborhood. The cool evening breeze was a gentle counterpoint to the lingering warmth of the day, carrying with it the distant hum of nightlife and the soft echoes of laughter from nearby streets. Our conversation meandered quickly between light-hearted memories and reflective pauses. We spoke quietly about our favorite moments of the day, our voices mingling with the nocturnal sounds of the city—a subtle lullaby that seemed to underscore both the fleeting nature of our time together and the enduring hope of future encounters. Though neither of us mentioned the heavy, unspoken truth of farewells, the silences between our words were filled with unexpressed longing and the bittersweet reality of temporary parting.

Later that night, we found solace on the worn, familiar couch, each of us cradling a cup of hot tea that seemed to warm our bodies and hearts. The hours slipped by in a gentle, timeless hush, our conversation stretching from playful recollections of childhood antics to half-formed daydreams about the future. I felt the secure weight of Jeff's arm around my shoulders, a silent reassurance that even as the world outside continued to change, we had found our sanctuary in that moment. Sleep beckoned, soft and insistent, yet I resisted its pull, unwilling to let this final night dissolve into the oblivion of a passing moment. Gratitude swelled within me—gratitude for the shared laughter, tender gestures, and unmistakable sense that life, however transient, was a series of beautiful, interconnected moments.

Beneath all the complexity of parting feelings, I sensed a gentle promise unfolding in the quiet spaces between our words. Beyond the looming flight back to the States and the uncertainties that the future held, there was an unspoken hope that the bonds of family and friendship might someday guide me back to Jeff's side. That fragile hope, warm and persistent like the embers of a fire, was enough for the moment. It kept my heart alight against the encroaching chill of goodbye—a promise that this farewell, though painful, was not an end but rather a pause in an ongoing story of connection and possibility.

In those final moments of the night, as we sat wrapped in the soft glow of lamplight and the rich aroma of our shared tea, every nuance of the evening felt imbued with meaning. Each whispered laugh, reflective silence, and every glance filled with unspoken understanding stitched together the fabric of an ephemeral and eternal interlude. The delicate balance of joy and sorrow coexisted with a quiet assurance that what we had experienced was authentic and transformative. And in that delicate interplay between memory and hope, I allowed myself to believe that the threads of our lives, though momentarily separated by distance and time, might one day weave back together again.

Thus, as the night deepened and our words slowly faded into the soft hum of the darkened room, I held onto the certainty that every farewell carries the promise of another meeting with it. The tender energy of those final two days in Johannesburg, with its vibrant market escapades, tranquil garden wanderings, spirited cricket match, and intimate shared moments, would remain etched in my heart—a cherished mosaic of experiences that, despite the inevitability of change, would forever sustain the hope of returning to Jeff's side in a future yet unwritten.

Chapter 12
Farewell...or Something More

Morning arrived in a gentle wash of golden light, the soft beams filtering through the lacy curtains of Jeff's living room and painting delicate patterns on the worn sofa where I had dozed off the previous night. I lay there for a long, languid moment, half awake and cradled by the warm embrace of sleep, my mind drifting through hazy recollections of the night before. The peaceful quiet of the house enveloped me—quite far removed from the clamorous world outside, where the busy hum of traffic or the harsh beeps of alarms had no place. In that serene sanctuary, the only sounds were the slow, rhythmic cadence of my breathing and the soft creak of wooden floorboards as Jeff moved about in the kitchen, preparing for the day with an unhurried grace.

For a blissful instant, I forgot that this was my final day in Johannesburg—the day that would carry me away on a plane bound for the United States. In that tender pause, I remembered the last few weeks when I had transformed from a hesitant traveler into someone who had found adventure and an unexpected sense of home in this vibrant city. More profoundly, I had found a home in Jeff. The thought swelled in my chest like a bittersweet melody, a reminder that every moment here had been steeped in love and discovery.

Before long, I heard the soft murmur of footsteps and the gentle clink of ceramic against porcelain as Jeff emerged into the living room doorway. His hair tousled as if he had run his fingers through it in a moment of tender disarray, and he carried two steaming mugs of freshly brewed coffee. A playful smile lit his eyes as he greeted me with a warm, teasing tone: "Morning, sleepyhead." Handing me a mug, he seemed to infuse the air with a familiar intimacy that made my heart flutter with joy and sorrow.

I accepted the cup delicately, inhaling the rich, earthy aroma that blended hints of roasted beans with a subtle trace of spice. As I took that first slow, lingering sip, the warmth of the coffee spread through me, mirroring the rising warmth of an affection that had grown too deep to be contained. "Morning," I whispered in return, my gaze fixed on the familiar contours of his face. In that shared moment, our eyes met with an intensity that needed no words—a silent conversation filled with promises of love, regret, and the bittersweet anticipation of a farewell.

Our day unfolded with an unhurried rhythm that seemed to slow down time. In the cozy intimacy of his kitchen, we lingered over breakfast, savoring each bite of freshly toasted bread and each sip of our second cup of coffee. As we ate, we reminisced, recalling our first encounters. I remembered how our paths had crossed at a bustling, crowded corner, the chaos of the city momentarily falling away as our eyes locked. Jeff had insisted on guiding me through the labyrinthine streets of Johannesburg with both care and gentle humor. With every shared story of those early days—the hidden corners of the city he had revealed to me, the quiet moments of laughter, and the unspoken understanding that had blossomed between us—I felt my heart cling tighter to the memory of our newfound intimacy.

Later that morning, we left the comforting warmth of his home and ventured into the fresh embrace of the outdoors. We strolled through a nearby park where the world seemed washed anew by dew and light. The grass under our feet was cool and damp with the residue of the early dawn, and nature's gentle welcome cushioned every step we took. Above us, the jacaranda trees swayed in a delicate dance with the breeze, their violet blossoms rustling like whispered secrets from the past. Arm in arm, we paused by a playground where the jubilant laughter of children filled the air—a sound so pure and unburdened that it momentarily pulled us from our bittersweet bubble of impending loss.

We continued our wander through the park until our curiosity led us to a small, charming bakery near a winding path. Its inviting façade, adorned with a hand-painted sign and windows dressed in lace curtains, beckoned us to step inside. We ordered a few delectable pastries and additional cups of coffee, opting for a spontaneous makeshift brunch imbued with the romance of our shared adventure. Seated on a weathered bench beneath a blooming jacaranda, we watched the world pass by—a parade of ordinary moments suddenly transformed into something extraordinary by our togetherness. With every bite and every shared glance, I felt the universe conspire to etch this day into my memory forever.

That day, time felt both fleeting and infinite, a paradox of emotion that made me wish to freeze every precious second. I longed to capture the laughter, the soft-spoken words, the glances that spoke volumes, and the feeling of Jeff's hand warm against mine. Yet the inexorable march of time reminded me that soon, I would have to return to a world far removed from this enchanting reality. With heavy hearts, we eventually retraced our steps back to his home, knowing that the moment had come to pack my luggage and face the inevitable journey to the airport.

On the Corner of Coetze and Klein

The drive to the airport was a study in quiet introspection. Jeff tried valiantly to maintain a light, casual atmosphere, turning on a cheerful radio station and tapping a gentle rhythm on the steering wheel as if to orchestrate a final symphony of our shared time. But beneath his playful veneer lay the unspoken truth of my impending departure—a truth that clung to us like a fragile mist, thickening the air with the weight of goodbye. With every mile ticked by on the road, the tension in my chest grew, as did the fear that these moments were slipping away too soon.

Then, as if guided by some silent intuition, Jeff steered us off the main road about fifteen minutes from the terminal and into the parking lot of a little roadside restaurant I had never noticed before. My heart skipped a beat in confusion. Surely, we needed to go to the airport without delay. Sensing my unspoken worry, Jeff parked the car, killed the engine, and turned to me with a tenderness that belied the seriousness in his eyes. "Let's have one last meal together," he said softly, his voice carrying the weight of a promise. "I don't want to rush through a goodbye."

I nodded, my throat too tight to form words as a lump of emotion rose within me. We found a cozy haven inside the restaurant that seemed to exist out of time. The space was quaint and homey, adorned with checkered tablecloths that spoke of simpler times and small vases overflowing with

161

wildflowers that added a splash of untamed color to every table. We chose a secluded corner booth that overlooked a dusty stretch of highway—a view that, despite its apparent ordinariness, somehow became charged with the magic of our shared solitude. In that quiet nook, every minute stretched out, and the space between us seemed to hum with an almost electric intimacy.

We ordered simple fare—freshly made sandwiches and cold drinks that glistened in the soft afternoon light—but neither of us could muster an appetite as our thoughts swirled around the moment's gravity. The silence between us was not empty but filled with a thousand unspoken words, each echoing with hope and the sorrow of impending parting. My eyes began to glisten with tears each time I tried to speak, a silent testament to the love that had grown so unexpectedly and powerfully in such a short time. Was this it? Was I indeed on the cusp of leaving behind the man who had transformed my life with his kindness, unwavering support, and effortless ability to make the ordinary seem magical?

After an eternity of shared silence and tender glances, Jeff reached across the table and gently took my hand. His touch was warm and steady—a silent anchor amidst the swirling storm of my emotions. "You know," he began softly, his voice low and intimate, "I've met plenty of people in my travels, seen countless faces, and heard many stories. But

I've never met anyone quite like you." His simple yet profound words reverberated within me, stirring feelings I had long thought were reserved for fairy tales and whispered dreams.

My heart pounded in my chest as I attempted to form a response, to articulate the deep connection I felt. But words failed me, choked off by the overwhelming surge of emotion. Seeing my struggle, Jeff did something that took my breath away. He reached into his jacket pocket with deliberate slowness, his eyes never leaving mine as he withdrew a small, velveteen box that glimmered with the promise of a new beginning.

"I know this may seem sudden," he said, his voice trembling ever so slightly—a delicate blend of vulnerability and courage. Sliding the box gently across the table, he nodded for me to open it, inviting me to partake in a sacred and transformative moment.

My fingers trembled as I lifted the lid and saw a handmade gold ring set with a champagne diamond that caught the light in a dazzling dance, sparkling with every subtle movement as if celebrating the beauty of our connection. A gasp escaped my lips, and tears welled in my eyes as I stared at the ring and then at Jeff, whose gaze filled with tender hope and a daring vulnerability.

He spoke softly, "Come back to Africa and be my wife?"

The man I had met on a bustling city street—a man who had quietly and irrevocably changed the course of my life—was now offering me a symbol of his love and a promise of a future together, a life replete with the kind of adventure and intimacy I had only dared to dream about.

For a long, suspended moment, time itself seemed to slow. A thousand thoughts raced through my mind: the vast distance between our worlds, the practicalities of immigration, the business waiting for me back in the States, and the complexities of merging two lives that had been so separate until now. And yet, none of those concerns held sway in the face of the overwhelming sincerity that radiated from him. My entire journey—a spontaneous leap into the unknown—had led me to this unbelievable juncture in a quiet roadside café, where love had revealed itself most unexpectedly and beautifully.

Struggling to find my voice amidst the surge of emotions, I finally managed to choke out his name—a word that seemed to encapsulate the entirety of my heart's longing. Holding his gaze with all the hope and vulnerability I could muster, I nodded, tears streaming as I whispered, "Yes. Yes, I'll come back." In that single, tender affirmation, the weight of my decision and the promise of our future coalesced into a luminous moment of shared destiny.

Jeff's relief was evident—a shaky, joyful laugh escaped him as he gently slipped the ring onto my finger. Our hands remained intertwined across the table, our fingers locked in a silent pledge of unity as tears mingled with laughter. In that intimate exchange, the future unfurled before us like a glorious tapestry, vibrant with possibility and woven from the threads of every joyful moment we had shared. Every smile, tear, and whispered promise came together to create a vision of a life that felt beautifully inevitable despite its uncertainties. We lingered over that final lunch as long as we dared, savoring every second as if it were a stolen fragment of eternity. But the inexorable march of time eventually forced our separation.

At the airport terminal, under the stark fluorescent lights and the low murmur of rolling suitcases, Jeff walked me as far as security would allow. Our final embrace was long and tight—a hug that carried the weight of every unspoken promise and every trembling hope that perhaps this was not an ending. "This isn't goodbye," he spoke softly into my hair, pressing his lips tenderly to my forehead in a gesture of continuity, believing that our love would defy distance and time.

With my heart clutched tightly in my throat and tears threatening to spill over, I reluctantly stepped away, my every step heavy with both sorrow and an abiding hope. I glanced back over my shoulder, catching one last glimpse of him standing there with his hands tucked into his pockets, his face illuminated by a hopeful smile that reassured me that our parting was only temporary. In that bittersweet moment, I understood with crystalline clarity that our story was far from over. As I navigated the labyrinthine corridors of the airport, the ring on my finger caught the light from overhead fluorescents, glinting like a beacon of promise—a tangible reminder of the next grand adventure awaiting me: a life with Jeff, built together in the country that had captured my heart.

Every step away from that final embrace was laden with the certainty that love, once kindled so profoundly, would always find its way back. The memory of that shared morning, the echo of his soft laughter, and the warm imprint of his hand in mine would carry me forward into a future where distances were only temporary and every farewell hinted at a joyful reunion. The promise encapsulated in that gold ring was not merely a symbol of commitment—it was an invitation to write a new chapter, a romance that transcended borders and defied the ordinary.

As I made my way through the bustling terminal, the cacophony of announcements and the shuffle of travelers around me seemed to fade into a distant murmur. In my heart, I clutched the delicate hope that had blossomed over the past weeks—a hope that whispered of shared mornings filled with golden light, quiet afternoons under blooming jacarandas, and countless evenings spent in the tender embrace of a love that felt as natural as breathing. The ring on my finger pulsed softly with each heartbeat, a constant reminder that something deeper and more enduring had taken root despite the imminent separation.

And so, as I stepped onto the jetway and felt the cool draft of the airplane corridor, I carried with me the memories of a fleeting romance and the promise of a future rich with love, adventure, and the soft, persistent glow of hope. In that moment of parting, every heartbeat, every whispered memory, and every silent tear came together to forge a bridge between what was and what was yet to be—a bridge that spanned continents, defied time, and celebrated the timeless, unyielding magic of genuine connection.

In the days and months that followed, as I navigated the complexities of my return to the States, the memory of that tender morning, the intimate laughter shared over a final meal, and the electrifying moment of a ring proposal in a roadside restaurant served as my guiding star—a beacon of love reminding me that sometimes, farewells are not endings at all but invitations to a new beginning. With every challenge and every triumph, I would remember that in life's unpredictability, our hearts had found a way to entwine, proving that true love—like the gentle glow of a sunrise—always heralds the promise of another day, another chance, another beautiful beginning.

Thus, as I embarked on that journey away from Jeff, my soul was buoyed by the conviction that our parting was not a final farewell but a delicate pause before the next chapter of our intertwined lives. The ring on my finger, sparkling with every light it caught, was my constant reminder that love, in all its passionate, unpredictable glory, was the one adventure worth embracing—an adventure that promised to bring us back together, no matter the distance or the passing of time.

The End

About the Author

Judi Moreo is a glob-
ally celebrated speaker,
entrepreneur, and artist
who has captivated au-
diences worldwide with
her storytelling and
motivational insights.
Over the years, she has
inspired countless indi-
viduals through her en-
gaging self-help books
and compelling histor-
ical fiction. Now, she
embarks on an exciting new journey with her first
romance novel.

Drawing on her extensive experience as a
dynamic entrepreneur and sought-after keynote
speaker, Judi has mastered the art of weaving
inspiration with practical wisdom. Her previous
self-help and historical fiction works have earned
her acclaim for their authenticity, passion, and
transformative power. Now, with her debut romance
novel, Judi ventures into a fresh genre where love,
resilience, and personal growth intertwine to create

heartfelt narratives that resonate with readers on a deep personal level.

Judi brings a unique blend of warmth, creativity, and insight to every project. Her ability to connect with audiences is evident on stage and in her writing, where she crafts stories that uplift, challenge and empower. Whether she's sharing her journey on international stages, engaging in intimate workshops, or writing captivating narratives, Judi's work is a testament to her unwavering commitment to helping others live their best lives.

Beyond her literary and speaking endeavors, Judi is an avid traveler and a lifelong learner. She finds inspiration in exploring diverse cultures, connecting with people from all walks of life, and discovering how love and resilience shape our experiences. When she's not writing or speaking, she immerses herself in art, nurturing new creative projects, or simply savoring the beauty of everyday moments.

Judi Moreo's life is a testament to the transformative power of storytelling and creative expression. Through her work, she reminds us that our journeys are about achieving success, making meaningful connections, and leaving a positive mark on the world. Her legacy is one of inspiration, courage, and the relentless pursuit of dreams—a legacy that continues to inspire all who have the pleasure of hearing her speak or reading her words.

With this, her first romance novel, Judi Moreo opens a new chapter in her creative journey— one that promises to stir the heart, ignite the imagination, and remind us that every story of love is a story worth telling. Join her as she explores the transformative power of love, and let her words inspire you to believe in the magic of new beginnings.

To contact the author, email: judi@judimoreo. com